...And Out Come The Toys

Matt Brandenburg

Copyright © 2025 by Matthew Brandenburg, Sleight of Hand Publishing

All rights reserved.

No part of this book may be reproduced in any form or by any electronic or mechanical means, including information storage and retrieval systems, without written permission from the author, except for the use of brief quotations in a book review.

Contents

Track 1

Justin Wilder escaped the edge of the pit, a sweaty mess. The final strains of *Lagwagon*'s *May 16* still ringing in his ears. He pushed past a few guys with mohawks, and spiky hair plastered to their heads, and scanned the crowd for his friends. His enemy thoughts teased him this was the last night he'd spend with them, and they weren't even around.

Out of nowhere, his friend Aaron barreled him over, laughing, and poking Justin's ribs.

"Damn that fucking rocked!" He said as he strutted to the bar area of Slugworth's.

Justin shuffled in Aaron's wake and yelled after him, "they killed it up there."

"Hell yeah," Aaron said. He nodded at the merch table. "Man, it's going to be so sick going on the road with Fishbone next week."

"Yeah..." Justin swore he was happy for his friend.

He beamed when he spied the two standing at a tall table in the corner. Waving her arms as she spoke, his best friend Cam was hard to miss with her buzzed leopard print-dyed head. Next to her was Michelle with her pink hair, faded green Army jacket and plaid mini skirt dancing to the music in her head.

Justin rushed up and hugged Cam, "What'd you think?"

"Fuck, they sound so good live," Cam said. "I was just telling Michelle that we'll have to listen to *Let's Talk About Feelings* on our ride up to Michigan Tech tomorrow."

A frown snuck on Justin's face. "Oh yeah, it's probably my favorite of theirs. Cam was the one to introduce me to them a few years back. She's always doing that."

"Hey, what about me? I got you into the fucking Boll-weevils," Aaron said.

"What the fuck is Vince doing?" Cam said.

They watched their lanky friend in his torn leather jacket push a jock into a trash can. Vince tossed an empty plastic cup before attempting to wipe off his stained jeans. He flipped the jock off as he stomped away. When he spotted Justin and the others, his face lit up and he skipped over to their table.

"Hey shitheads, what's going on?"

"Oh, you know, watching you causing trouble," Cam said.

"Dude spilled my beer."

Justin couldn't help but wonder if after all of the shows they've been to, would this be the last one they went to together? "God, it sucks you all are leaving. I kinda wish there were more bands playing or something."

Vince put a finger up. "I've got an idea. One last hurrah before you bastards leave me with this mopey idiot."

They waited for Vince to continue.

"I think we finally go to the one place we haven't broken into yet, the one place that's haunted our town for years."

"You don't mean..." Cam said.

Vince flicked the round button on Justin's chest that guaranteed Challis' toys are 100 percent magic. "Hell yeah. Let's break into Challis' Factory and see if the rumors are true."

Aaron snorted, "you mean the heaps of cash?"

"I mean let's see if the fucking place is haunted, you dumbass."

Justin's face reddened as he glanced at his Converse and mumbled, "could be something fun to do, and you know, give you something to think about when you're up north or across the country or whatever."

"Yeah, sure, let's do it," Cam said while smirking. "One last fucked up adventure to cap off the summer, right?"

She leaned into him and whispered, "hey, I'll even let you pick the songs we listen to on the way, any track you'd like, I won't complain."

Frenetic energy zigzagged through Justin. The beating of the bass drum up on stage thundered in his chest. They turned when the cheers intensified. Tony Sly, the lead singer of *No Use For a Name*, walked up to the mic. Justin grabbed his friends. Then Tony said exactly what Justin was thinking, the perfect starting gun for the night.

"Let's get this fucking show started!"

Track 2

Darkness cloaked the abandoned toy factory. Before it closed ten years ago, it produced joy for millions of children. Now, the building on the outskirts of town squatted amongst scraggly trees, broken eighteen wheelers, and crooked light poles as lost as the toys it used to produce. Justin stared up at the entrance. He prayed there'd be cool shit in there, anything to make their last time together the best night of their lives.

His friends stood by him, ripples of excitement and awe radiating off them. He didn't know if it was the allure of breaking into the infamous landmark, Vince's silly rumors of a hidden vault in the factory, or they felt sorry for him, but they agreed to come along.

Stains coated the slate gray walls broken up with boxy windows near the top. Crooked dead trees blocked the building's lower half. Smokestacks sprouted out of it like a body stuck with daggers. Extensive stone steps, with a red carpet running up the middle like a tongue, led to a landing and a ridiculous sized door that could have been stolen from a gothic cathedral. Columns of twisted, stained marble held up a pitched roof above the entrance. The longer they stood there, the more Justin noticed the garish smiles on molded superheroes, baby dolls with puckered lips, dopey dogs, and boxy robots peering from the wall around the door.

Aaron chuckled as he slipped the hood of his *Gangster Fun* hoodie off his head. His brown eyes flashed in the slight moonlight. "What the fuck man?"

"This dude was something else." Cam played with the dull stud in her nose.

"I can't even imagine what it would have been like visiting this place." Michelle said while digging a cigarette out of her jacket. The chains hanging off her skirt jingled as she moved. "Those five kids that won the contest must have been freaked the fuck out and super stoked at the same time."

A breeze whistled over the barren parking lot behind them and bit at their skin. Dead leaves skittered over broken pavement, whispering legends. Rumors had bounced around Justin's school playground and, later, the bars he snuck into, about what it'd be like to witness the factory's magic. Challis, the whimsical owner, kept the place off limits for visitors, and no one knew anyone that worked there. They all remembered the thrill and jealousy knowing those children were the first people in the world to enter the factory. It all curdled when the winners never came out.

Cam went up the steps first. The back of her hoodie revealed a large patch for *Operation Ivy*, the skanking man outlined in white. Her Doc Martens barely made a sound as she climbed to the top. Justin's eyes welled as they followed her up and he dreaded what life was going to be like without her. They'd been like siblings since the sixth grade when she taught him *Agent Orange* was a better version of

The Offspring. When she reached the landing, she flipped them off with a smirk and disappeared into the shadows.

"Oh man, this place is giving me the creeps," Aaron said.

Vince's leather jacket crinkled as he turned, safety pins clicking together. "Dude it's just an old fucking building, where's the fucking tough guy that beat the shit outta that redneck that called you a nigg—"

Justin coughed, cutting Vince off, and eyed him with a pleading expression to take it down a peg.

Aaron's jaw tightened for a moment before he laughed. "That bastard was all tough until he had my boot up his ass. Anyway—"

A piercing scream from the top of the stairs severed Aaron's sentence.

The terror in the yell sent Aaron booking toward the sound. The others were seconds behind. Chasing after Aaron, he prayed a rat had spooked Cam or she was playing a joke. *At least Aaron's almost up there, nothing scares him, and if it is a prank, he won't be able to not laugh.* Justin appreciated the way they had each other's backs. The feeling soured when he realized that wouldn't be true anymore.

"Motherfucker!" Cam said.

The air around the factory thickened. Scuffling boots, wispy flutters, and clicking bounced amongst the columns. Someone grunted. Justin's skin tightened, energy coursed up his spine. He broke through the shadows with Vince and Michelle.

Aaron stood in front of Cam, one of his fists up while he pointed at the darkness. Cam snarled and squinted as she tried reaching over Aaron's shoulder, her hand a claw ready to grab whatever had upset her.

"Stay the fuck over there you piece of shit!" Aaron said.

"What's going on?" Justin said.

"I was at the door, testing the handle, when this bastard came creeping out of the shadows like a perv." Cam said as her cheeks flushed.

Heaped against the wall were ripped open stacks of garbage bags with ribbons, tablecloths, and busted toys spilling out. The stench of rotten food and decaying vegetation permeated the landing.

Justin jumped when the pile moved. "What the hell?"

The heap rose. Colorful glitter and sparkly strips of plastic fluttered to the ground. Two green orbs glowed near the top.

"Oh, howdy my children! It's so good to see you!" The voice emerged from the pile in a high falsetto, a faint echo warped and bent the sound into a chorus. A slight ticking and static punctuated the greeting, "I hope you are excited to play in the toy room, it is so much fun!"

"The fuck..." Vince said.

They took a step back as the pile moved into a slice of moonlight. Broken parts of toy cars and plastic limbs tumbled to the ground in a clatter. On top of its oblong head sat a floppy fedora. A string of doll heads with ruby eyes hung from its neck. Justin blinked a few times. The face was instantly recognizable from childhood memories, t-shirts, even a grinning poster still hanging on Justin's wall: Challis. *He can't be alive, can't be sleeping on the front steps of his own factory.* Despite the blue marks zigzagging across his face, the electric orange hair that appeared to be made of plastic, the glowing green eyes, it was clearly Challis.

The crunch of breaking plastic and sizzle of electricity echoed as the owner took a wobbly step forward. His body flopped back and forth like it was made of rubber.

"Now, before you go, I must warn you, do not be afraid of the little ones. It's been forever since they've had any new friends to play with. Any that do come never leave, that's how much fun they have!" It finished by burping out rapid-fire laughter.

What the hell is happening? Justin's scalp tightened. *Are they going to want to keep going now?*

He let out a breath, working up the courage to speak, when Vince sucker punched the person on the side of their head.

"Get the fuck out of here!" Vince said.

The stranger crumpled against the wall. His hat floated down onto the pile of garbage. Vince grimaced as he studied the open cuts on his knuckles.

"What the fuck are you doing, Vince?" Michelle asked, adding in a whisper, "God, didn't he look like Challis?"

Justin perked up. *So, I'm not the only one that thought that.*

"I'm not going to let some crackhead bastard mess with us, especially one dressed up like that. Fuck him."

Yeah, but did you have to knock him unconscious? Justin glanced at Vince, wishing he had the nerve to call his friend out. *Why is he the one staying?*

"Uh, so what the hell do we do now?" Aaron asked.

"Fucking leave him. Who cares?" Vince said.

"But what if you killed him or something? We should probably get him help," Michelle said as she chewed on a fingernail and paced.

Cam tiptoed to the body, "Why the hell would he dress up like Challis, and what's up with his face? Vince couldn't have split his skin that bad."

Vince rubbed his knuckles, glared at Cam, then went to the door, "And say what exactly? We just happened to be up here and found this strange dude hiding in the garbage? Fuck that."

"Yeah, but what if someone finds him? Are they going to come—"

Before Michelle could finish, the person leapt into the air. It landed behind Vince, its arms and legs stretched out.

Dark green eyes flashed and rolled in their sockets. A wicked grin grew until it threatened splitting the pink face, revealing more of the dark blue beneath. Vince flattened against the door, his mouth hanging open. The group stood transfixed as the man shuddered and bounced.

Its voice crackled and slowed like a warped tape, "Oh yes, they'll love to play with all of you. We are all going to have so much fun!"

The bizarre man sprung over them and landed on the stairs. He pranced to the ground before heading to the building's east side. "I can't wait, the gate is almost open!"

Justin's pounding heart drowned out the others' frantic breathing. He didn't want this to be the final note his friends left on. They needed to have a good time, something to remind them of the fun they used to have as a group, and how nothing would compare to what they had together. If this soured the night and caused them to leave, would it taint their other memories? Would they want to come back to him next summer?

"So, that fucking happened," Aaron said.

"What the hell? Fuck, this was fun and all, but I'm not about to run into another damn crackhead, no thanks." Michelle touched Justin's shoulder, "Dude, I know you really want to do this, but the alcohol is wearing off, and we all have a long day tomorrow. I really appreciate you wanting to have one last big thing, but I promise, we aren't that far away, and well, Cam and I wanted to surprise you with—"

"Fuck, really?" Justin threw his hands up before stomping to the edge of the landing. "Come on! We are standing right on the fucking doorstep. When did you all worry so much about a shithead? Or getting some sleep? We used to stay up all night at shows and afterparties."

Gritting his teeth, he kept his back to his friends so they wouldn't see his tears.

"Actually, I am a little interested in seeing what's in there," Cam said.

"But..." Michelle said.

"Yeah, Justin's right, it was just some fucker, we could have taken him." Aaron patted Justin on the back. "One last fucked up adventure, right?"

Cam nudged her future roommate. "It'll be fine, we can sleep when we get up there. Besides, it's not like this'll take all night."

Vince laughed, punched the door, and with wild eyes gazed at the others. "Fucking A, let's do this!"

Vince slipped out a flask and passed it around. Cam took a swig, winked at the group, then grabbed the door handle. Justin wiped his mouth, wishing he'd been the one to open the door. When she pushed, it didn't budge. She tried pulling and nothing happened. Panic gripped Justin's chest and filled his head with worries they wouldn't be able to get in. As he scrambled for another plan, Cam shifted to a flat space between carvings of miniature lanky armed children and toy cars, put her shoulder in place, and pushed. *At least she didn't give up.* He wondered if he'd have kept trying. A flash of the multiple times he gave up doing homework, playing the guitar, applying for community college ran through his thoughts. The door creaked and moved an inch. Sweat slicked her forehead, her mouth in a grimace, a growl slipping between her teeth.

"There's something really heavy behind this."

"Alright everyone, teamwork and all that shit," Aaron said as he made his way next to Cam. Vince and Michelle took a final swig from the flask and found a spot to help.

Justin's head bowed when he realized he was the last one, then he squeezed in between Michelle and Cam. He wanted to be like Aaron, confident and cool, but he was positive he'd come across as an idiot or say the wrong thing. Putting his hands on the door, he felt the bite of splinters on its surface. Cam counted and they all heaved. Something behind the door scraped against the floor followed by the clatter of items tumbling down. They grunted with each push. Their Docs and Converse struggled to gain traction. After what felt like forever, the door slid open. They flopped into the factory in a heap.

Aaron jumped up first. He dusted himself off and offered to help Cam. Vince grumbled he was closer. Michelle picked at a bit of glass stuck into her palm as she stood. A pang of being forgotten spiked Justin's thoughts when no one helped him.

Light sneaking in through the greasy windows allowed them their first glimpse at the inside of Challis' Toys.

Track 3

"God," Justin said as he stepped over a heap of broken furniture.

"It looks like...shit," Cam said.

The T-shaped lobby with gray stone walls and floors didn't scream the magical toy factory Justin had imagined. His friends spread out, weaving through piles of busted up coffee tables and chairs with their stuffing strewn about. Overhead lights hung from the ceiling like dead spiders. Bags of garbage were tossed all over the place, their contents of moldy food and paper created amorphous shapes in the gloom. Their shoes stuck to tacky puddles coating the floor. Water dripping somewhere gave the area the feeling of a cave.

"Damn, you think this is from the celebration?" Aaron said as he held up part of a moldy banner. The letters W, E, and L in red and blue font were all that was left. Copper colored splatters were on the white background.

"Maybe, I mean, check that shit out." Michelle pointed toward the back of the lobby, the bottom part of the T, which appeared to go on forever. Half of another banner hung from the ceiling, empty wrinkled balloons swaying from it, with the words …come play with m… on the filthy canvas. She glanced at the others. "What the hell happened here?"

"Maybe they had to get out in a rush?" Cam said while poking a stack of gift bags.

No one wanted to say she was right, that the employees and Challis probably booked it out of town to avoid getting arrested.

Justin maneuvered his way to the lobby's center, where Vince was digging through the remains of a front desk. Warped brochures, paper plates with decayed bugs and crumbs, and scorch marks covered the glass top. Toys with joyful faces had been built into the desk's front. He leaned over to check on what Vince was doing. Pictures of kids and a dog were on one end of a blocky computer. His friend flipped through papers, concentration masking his face.

"What are you looking for?"

Vince glanced up for a second, "A ma—"

"Fuck, look!" Aaron said and lifted two toys. In one hand he held a shark wearing a red bandana, green camo pants, a six-pack torso, and two machine guns in its muscled arms. In the other, a mold-coated stuffed penguin. One of its eyes in a permanent wink while the other one hung down its cheek. "Do you think it'll still talk?"

"Ha, imagine the crazy shit it'd say," Cam said. "The cassette tape is probably warped to hell; it'd sound like it was raising a demon."

"I can't believe all of this shit has been here. That was what ten years ago? I'm surprised it hasn't all been stolen." Michelle kicked a folding table out of her way. "Oh fuck, there's still nasty ass cake on this one!"

"Yeah, March seventh, nineteen-eighty-seven, at ten in

the morning those fucking kids went in," Justin said. He did his best to suppress the idea those children ruined this wonderful place for him.

"Dude, you had that date on the tip of your tongue, didn't you?" Michelle said, shaking her head.

"Did you never notice that pin on his hoodie?" Aaron said while shuffling through a pile of broken action figures, picking out two halves of a green and black torso. "Where'd you get that Challis Seal of Quality pin anyway?"

"Some dude made a bunch and was selling them outside of Flipside Records," Justin said, touching the pin with the starburst and childish lettering promising the toy was made with 100% magic, the seal featured on all of Challis' Toys packaging.

"Oh, that was probably Rick. I think he'd found a bunch of brochures like these," Vince said as he held up a crinkled booklet. "I'm sure I even saw some of them up at Lamplighter's a year or two ago. I bet someone's got a bunch of this shit in their basement waiting to sell it off."

"You think it's worth something?" Justin asked. People were always into creepy shit. A plan to snag some on the way out formed in the back of his head.

"Probably. But there's gotta be more here. I know we didn't see the guards, but I know they're here..." Vince bent out of Justin's view, followed by a metallic screech and the rustling of papers.

When Vince didn't say anything else, Justin meandered toward the left side of the lobby. Long tears were cut into the walls, *almost like claw marks*. A cold feeling settled over him and his skin prickled. He whipped around. Aaron continued playing with the shattered toys. Michelle and Cam were facing the back hall, whispering. Opposite from him, he spotted a diminutive shadow swaying. After a heartbeat of studying it, he convinced himself it was a pile of garbage and wandered back to the center of the lobby.

"...and you don't just pack up and leave without forgetting something," Vince said.

Justin glanced over at the girls. "Hey, Michelle, Vince is agreeing with you, it's a fucking miracle!"

Cam and Michelle laughed as Vince made a jerk off motion. As they weaved through the debris, a slight pang of jealousy tugged at Justin's heart.

"...days before classes start, we should totally check out that one place," Michelle said.

"Oh yeah, I heard Waldo's is pretty rad. There's that record shop too." Cam smiled. "It's crazy to think about being that far north, I kinda want to take some pictures of the lake."

"Do you think the water's freezing all the time?" Michelle said as they reached the front desk.

As happy as Justin was for his friends getting to do big things, he hated how it reminded him he wasn't. Why couldn't they all keep doing stupid fun stuff together forever?

Michelle eyed Justin and Vince. "You all know I'm always fucking right. So, are we going to keep moving?"

"In just a damn minute, I'm trying to find a map or something."

"What for? Aren't we just going to wander around and look at shit?" Aaron said, dropping the toys he was playing with.

"You know what for. That fucking vault."

"For real? You really do believe that, don't you?"

Justin cringed. Anytime he mentioned the secret vault, they'd laugh and pretend to agree with him. Of course,

Challis would leave behind a bunch of money in the shut-down factory.

"Yes, you fuckhead. Look around, this fucking place looks like they left in a damn hurry. Don't you laugh, because when I find that shit, you aren't getting any of it. You can enjoy your time being the bands' bitch. They probably won't even remember your name half the time."

Aaron stepped to Vince. Their eyes burning holes in each other. The dripping of water and a slight tapping filled the lobby. A shadow flitted across a wall.

Cam sighed. "Are you done? It's not about either of you tonight, so quit comparing dicks and let's do this. Besides our only option right now is this very long and disturbing hallway, so who the fuck needs a map?"

The two continued the stare down.

"Guys, we can't keep doing this shit. Not tonight. We're in the damn factory! How fucking cool is that? It'll be just like old times! Besides, what does it hurt to maybe have a goal?" Justin's mouth felt like it'd been stuffed with socks, his skin burning, his mind running a million miles as it questioned if Aaron would be mad at him. He didn't want to side with Vince, all he wanted was to keep them moving.

The two didn't budge, though their shoulders loosened. Vince cracked a grin. "Hey man, it's all good. Justin is right, won't hurt to check, will it?"

"Yeah, it's cool." Aaron said as he picked up a piece of paper. He crinkled it into a ball and tossed it at Vince. "Maybe then I can say I told you so."

Vince forced a laugh that gained an echo in the lobby's far corner. Everyone turned.

"This place is a little freaky, right?" Michelle said. "Like there's something watching us."

"It's just all the broken toys. The place has been sitting

here vacant forever, I'm sure there's some structural issues." Aaron wiggled his arms and whispered, "or maybe it's the ghost of Challis eager to play with you."

"Fuck off!" Michelle said as she scanned the room, her arms wrapped around her body. "Everyone knows the dude was freakin' nuts. We don't even need to talk about setting up some crazy ass contest for a *special* tour. Just look at some of his fucked-up toys, total nightmare fuel. Then there's the fact no one ever came in here. Why do you think he kept it so secret? Something messed up was here."

The others glanced at each other. Justin worried she was losing her nerve and would bail. Would Cam follow? The last few weeks the two had been attached at the hip planning their big move to Michigan Tech. If they both left the factory, would Aaron stick around, especially if Vince stayed?

"God, I remember being in the crowd at the gates here," Cam said. She picked up a soggy stuffed bunny, its polyester fur clumped with black stains. "Staring up at this building being pissed I wasn't one of the five. I just kept wondering what it'd be like to be in here, a place where you could be whomever you wanted to be without fear."

Memories of being ten and sitting in front of the TV watching the news floated through Justin's mind. His imagination had built this astonishing story about the new toys the contest winner played with, the ones he'd never get. Part of him had dreamt that if he'd won, Challis would offer him the chance to stay at the factory. The owner would move him and his parents out of the cramped apartment, way from the bills, and constant nights alone while they worked.

Cam tossed the bunny. "When the doors opened and he appeared, it was like peeking into heaven. Those unlucky bastards had no idea what they were in for. Fuck, neither did any of us."

Justin shambled from the group. He toyed with the Challis button on his hoodie. "God, when those damn kids went into the factory, and the gates closed, I just sat there with Svengoolie on the TV. I knew the stories they were going to tell were going to be beyond anything we could imagine."

Cam leaned against the wall with her hands in her pockets. "Yeah, it was going to be wild."

"Then College Football came on. There was nothing about them leaving, remember? I kept picturing what they were doing. The place looked so damn huge, how long were they going to be in there? Here, I mean. Maybe they were going to spend the night, fuck, how cool would that have been? Fucking killed me knowing I'd missed that chance." Justin kicked some toy cars, their metal bodies skittering over the floor. "It wasn't until the next day we started hearing about something not being right. Then, what, a week later we hear the place is closing? They didn't even apologize. No more fucking toys, nothing."

"Fuck it, let's go," Vince said. "I can't find shit on this desk."

"You mean they don't have a map that says hidden money here?" Aaron asked.

"I thought they'd have a map for employees or something, asshole."

The thought of taking charge became sharp icicles in Justin's veins. He motioned toward the hallway. "Welp, let's rock and see what we find."

Track 4

Tile floors, dark walls, and a ceiling so far above they couldn't make out where it ended, made up the corridor. Silence pressed down on them. Justin hoped the darkened hall, or the tingling sensation of being watched, kept them from talking and it wasn't them regretting their decisions to come here. Michelle hugged her arms tighter around her stomach. Shadows crept toward the group.

As he led the way, something scraped against his arms.

"What the hell?" he said.

"Uh, did the walls move? Or am I still fucking drunk?" Aaron said. "Can you see anything in front of you?"

Justin squinted. Traces of moonlight reflected off the walls, offering nothing more than a vague sense of space. Behind him, the flick of a lighter, the whiff of butane. A quick glance over his shoulder revealed the glow of a Zippo in Michelle's hand. It struggled with the dark around them. The path continued forward, with a slight incline rising into the distance.

"What the fuck is going on?" Cam said.

Justin scrunched up his face as he took in the entrance to the hall framing her. It appeared wider and lower than where they were standing.

Michelle let out a laugh. "It's an optical illusion."

"Jeezus," Cam said.

"This place is so fucking wild," Justin smirked. "Can you imagine what other weird shit we are going to find?"

"Can you imagine walking through this fucking fun house hallway every day for work?" Cam said under her breath.

As they continued, the walls and ceiling crowded them until they had to walk single file. Michelle's lighter reflected off the hint of a small door. Each step made it shrink more. *Fuck, I led them toward a dead end. Bet it wouldn't have happened if someone else was up front.*

"So, uh, did any of you see a door that's not fake anywhere?" He wiped sweat off his forehead.

"Nope, not a fucking—" A whoosh of hot air cut Cam off.

Justin jumped as the wall to his right slid away revealing a new hall. A string of spotlights marked a path through the corridor of no right angles and bulging walls. Bright primary color polka dots covered the surfaces. On the right side a line of bulbous round objects sprouted from the walls. Children's laughter filled the space, yet the years of abandonment warped and twisted the glee into something haunting and inhuman. Justin's nerves tingled with excitement.

"Well, whatever it is, it's better than standing here with our fucking thumbs up our asses," Vince said.

Hushed breaths followed Justin as he entered.

The lights and wacky angles added shadows and messed with his vision. The floor sank under his weight, giving him pause until he realized it was coated with a spongy material. When he passed the first round object on the wall he did a double-take.

"Holy shit, what the fuck is that?" Cam said, the horrified expression on her face matching his.

A baby's head coated in silver stared at them. Below bugged out eyes and chubby cheeks, was a gaping mouth that could have swallowed Justin's fist. Two blocky teeth jutted out of the bottom gums. Beneath flaking silver paint, were dull pinks and browns.

"Touch it," Aaron said.

"Fuck, are you serious?" Cam said.

"Well, there's no way it's a real head, right? So, it's gotta be plastic or something. Just do it."

"You fucking do it," she said.

"Fine, whatever." He squeezed through the others to get closer.

Aaron raised his hand up to the head. A slight tremor vibrated his outstretched finger as he hesitated. Vince nudged him. Justin winced, imagining the finger going right through the skull and into the desiccated brain. The flesh on the side of the baby's head dented in before popping back into place.

"It's plastic." Aaron wrapped the head in his fist. "Fucking hell, this is super weird."

They released a collective sigh.

"Okay, shit. That is something," Justin said.

"How the fuck is this supposed to be fun for kids?" Cam asked.

More heads lined their shuffling path. Each one had a slightly different expression, except for the mouths. Those were all open and ready to swallow a baseball, their two front teeth eager to sink deep into the leather. Justin's scalp crawled under the babies' gaze. His friends mumbled as they jostled into his back. Ahead, the hall turned to the left. Anticipation carried him forward. He skidded to a stop when Aaron yelped.

"Fucking head bit me," he said as he shook a finger.

"What the hell are you–" Before Justin could finish, the heads began chomping at the air. A loud ticking matched the baby's mastication. The group inched back against the wall.

"Why the hell did you put your hand in their mouth? Fuck, dude," Michelle said.

"Okay kids, keep your hands and feet away from the babies, they might be hungry," Vince said.

Squeezing together, they followed the bend to the left.

They entered a square empty room. A child's bed stacked with five teddy bears had been painted on the right wall. The stuffed animals were smiling, though the mirth didn't match the sinister glint in their eyes, the teeth pushing through the cotton. A window with a beautiful painted landscape was above the bed: a neighborhood, the sky bright blue. On their left, a mural of a dresser with robot toys on top, along with some bookshelves. Something buzzed and Michelle screamed. A few mobiles dropped from the ceiling and started spinning the baby ducks and rabbits hanging from their arms. Dead bugs and dust sprinkled down on them. Besides the opening they had entered, there wasn't an exit, only a door painted on the wall.

"This place is seriously messing with my head," Michelle said through a hand covering her mouth. "Why is it like a funhouse?"

"Who the fuck knows?" Aaron said.

"Is there any way out of here?" Cam said.

Justin approached the fake door and knocked. "Nope."

"I think we missed something; this is just a dead end," Aaron said while touching the walls.

"No way, I'm not going back through that hall of heads." An edge of worry crusted Michelle's words.

Fuck. Please, there has to be something. Justin scanned the walls. "Maybe there's a secret button or switch hidden in one of the pictures. Challis put this here for a reason."

For a few minutes the susurrus of skin rubbing against the walls and the whirling tick of the heads opening and closing their mouths filled the room. Justin tried imagining what those kids went through as he dragged his fingers over painted books. Did they feel the same excitement and eagerness to see what was around the next corner? He forgot all about what tomorrow would bring, the pain of being alone and facing a dead-end future. All that mattered was being here with his friends and exploring a dream.

Lost in his happiness, he jolted when Cam sucked air through her teeth after a loud click.

"Found something." Her finger pressed against one of the teddy bear's noses. Next to Justin, the wall shuddered.

"Okay, I guess try the other noses," he said.

Each of them stepped in front of a bear and pushed its nose. A fanfare of xylophones, triangles, and tin whistles went off. Then the fake door slid open with a clockwork tick.

A wall of darkness greeted them. The group jostled and pressed against each other, forcing Justin forward.

"Hey, wait a sec, what the fuck are you all doing?"

"It's not me! Something's pushing me," Vince said.

Straining against the group, he tried to stop. The last thing he needed was to run into a hole or trip into a bunch of garbage. But it was too late, he was through the door.

The dark felt heavy and soupy. An echo accompanied

their racket. In the distance came the faint gurgle of water. There was a sense of space, an emptiness at odds with the cramped hallways and room they had gone through. Beside him came the heavy breathing and mutterings of his friends.

As he reached for Michelle's lighter, lights flicked on overhead.

Track 5

Once the purple and blue spots faded from his vision, he had to tell himself he wasn't dreaming. His friends stood on either side of him, frozen, eyes sucking it all in, mouths searching for the right words.

"Oh my god. What is this?" Cam said in a whisper.

"It's beautiful," Michelle said.

The massive space held green hills, lush trees, giant flowers, and twisting pathways. Blue skies and fluffy white clouds painted on the ceiling almost completely hid the pipes, wires and air vents crisscrossing the area. A mixture of sinus burning chemicals, mold, swamp, and shit hung in the air. Life-sized dollhouses, army forts, and superhero hideouts lined the walls. The structures dwarfed them; they could have been action figures waiting to be played with. Every object bent, twisted, or curved to keep reality at bay.

All Justin could think was they had stepped into a magical fairyland. Then a better description came to mind: the ultimate toy room.

They floated forward as if beckoned, barely noticing the door whooshing closed behind them. Their eyes darted across the room; their minds drunk on all the wonders. A path of wooden blocks snaking through trees and a neon green meadow, summoned them to explore.

Like slowly realizing you have something in your teeth, garbage bags, torn cardboard boxes, and pieces of office furniture corrupted the pristine dream. Areas under the trees, on hilltops, and on the outskirts of the grassy area held bunkers and improvised cover of junk. Toys peered from behind the barriers and trunks of trees.

"This is fucked. What the hell happened?" Aaron asked.

Cam lifted her arms and dropped them. "Shit, I don't know. Maybe it was part of the contest? Maybe someone was packing and then decided to play a game or something?"

Michelle crept ahead, her eyes shining. "It's too bad, this place is like a dream."

She loves it! Justin's chest warmed. His worry about coming here melted. Maybe they'd want to come back next summer, they could make it a yearly tradition.

"Holy shit, they have the whole set of Shark Commandos!" Aaron took off into the woods.

The spell broke and everyone ran in different directions. Aaron picked up a bunch of muscly shark action figures and played with them, building elaborate scenes from the show tied to the toys. Michelle waltzed between trees and up a hill, her head tilted, her arms out, her Army jacket billowing. Cam put her hands into the pockets of her hoodie and trudged through neon pink grass. She bent and picked up a purple monster with one oversized eye. Even

Vince seemed enthralled, his boots clicking on the path as he stared at the trees and ceiling. Justin explored while keeping an eye on them, tattooing this memory to his brain.

When he crested a hill, he found Cam collecting stacks of Challis' stuffed monster line. He paused when he noticed a tear slipping down her cheek.

"Hey, you okay?" There'd only been a few times when he saw her cry. Usually tied to shitheads at a show or school that'd fuck with her.

Cam wiped her nose with the sleeve of her hoodie. "I always wanted to get these when I was younger. Do you remember the commercials? They'd be walking through a village, pretending to be what the others thought was normal, when no one was around they'd transform into what they really were. They'd smile and join others like them in the woods, dancing and being happy. We couldn't afford them. And now look at them, just piled here like garbage."

One thing he'd learned spending time with Cam was she didn't share when she didn't want to. Part of why they got along so well. They each had their own ways to compartmentalize, only letting the pressure free when they were ready. She never asked him about why he was staying on her couch, or why he showed up places starving and wearing dirty clothes. He didn't ask her when she started showing up their junior year of high school in dresses and makeup. Most of their sharing and opening up came from whatever CD or tape they'd play. It was easier to explain themselves with a track from *No Use For A Name* or *The Get Up Kids* than using words. Unfortunately, Justin didn't have any music to help him speak now.

"Fuck, what's stopping you from taking one of these

things? But, look, you are who you are meant to be, and hey, *we're* in the woods. Look at Michelle, she's already dancing. We are already halfway there. Forget all that other shit."

"I don't know. This place...it feels off. I mean, why is the power on? And, like if I took one of these, would I be cursed? Is that what happened to the others?"

He glanced at the lights, struck by her question.

"Who knows? Maybe this is why Vince's security guards are out there? But, anyway, it's a bit crazy seeing all of this isn't it? Not in a million years did I think it'd be like this."

Cam grabbed a sad stuffed bear. She pushed the legs in, twisted the body around until it turned into a monstrous squid with a wicked grin. "I am happy we came here. I know you were worried about stuff, but you gotta know we have a p—"

"Don't worry about it. Let's just enjoy now and pretend tomorrow doesn't exist. What's that Pennywise track? Something about living every day like it was your last? Let's do that." He stood and twisted his back. "Keep playing, I'm going to check things out, maybe there's a toy here for me."

He strutted further down the path. He didn't need her catching the hurt tightening his jaw. Over every hill, behind every tree, were new discoveries. There was no need to grow up and be an adult, no need to worry about a pointless life with no future, no need witnessing his friends move on while he was stuck.

"Hey guys, check this out!" Aaron's voice brought him back to reality.

"Whoa, this is crazy!" Cam said.

Justin found his friends standing near a filthy pond he thought was bigger than the school's football field. Fake sand lined the edge, bits of soggy paper and cloth clumped together in places. White froth and bubbles slid across the brown sludgy surface, rainbow-like stains swirled in places. A mechanical stench roiled off the pond. His scalp prickled and something told him they should keep exploring.

"God, the stink is the only thing that makes this seem real," Aaron said.

Vince picked up a spaceman action figure and tossed it into the water.

"What the fuck did you do that for?" Aaron asked.

Vince picked his nose. "Why not? It's not like it matters."

"So...I think I'm ready to see the next awesome thing here." Justin scooted from the pond and studied the walls. "You think there's a door?"

"There's fucking doors everywhere," Vince said while motioning at the wall-sized playsets.

"Okay. I guess one of those has to lead out of here."

Leaving the pond behind, they fanned out.

"Don't forget, there might be a hidden switch or something," Cam said.

Like Vince had said, there was a doorway or cave opening everywhere along the walls. The paths were no help either, they went in all directions. Which door did they use to enter the toy room? None of them looked familiar. Challis must have wanted the kids guessing and forced to follow him on his own timeline. Maybe that's why they went missing, they didn't listen to factory owner's directions. A sick thrill and gut twisting worry buzzed in his stomach as he imagined being trapped here.

Justin picked a pink Victorian dollhouse in front of him, hoping for the best. He climbed the two short steps onto the squat porch and jiggled the white door. The handle spun useless in his grip. Following Cam's advice, he tested the doorbell, felt the wooden column, picked at the wood siding, checked under the porch.

"Any luck?" he called out.

"Fuck no. But I did find a kick ass plastic dart gun." Aaron laughed. "No darts, but still fucking rad."

"There's gotta be something," Cam said, followed by the thud of her boot as she kicked a door. "Why. Won't. You. Open!"

"Maybe it's stuck?" Vince said.

Justin ambled to a rocky castle and spotted Michelle bent over the water.

"Hey, Michelle, what are you doing?" he asked, picturing what might be in the disgusting pond.

She stuck her hand in. "There's something in here, maybe it's a button."

"I wouldn't put my hand in there, who knows what shit is in there," Cam said as she continued to kick.

"Can almost touch it."

Near the middle of the pond a circle of bubbles broke the surface. The hairs on Justin's neck went rigid. He stepped toward her, his eyes on the churning water sliding closer to Michelle.

"Get your hand out of—"

A jet of water exploded straight up.

An actual-size version of one of *Gavin the Warrior*'s terrible monsters towered over them, almost touching the ceiling. Stubby legs connected to each segment of the monster's red and black centipede-like body wiggled. Its joints clicked with every move. Dirty pond water dripped off its dull skin. It curled its body into an S shape. Cracks in its shell revealed machinery and a squirming blue mass. At the top sat a round head covered in a white and red circular mask, large pinchers near a long thin mouth clacking together. The stench of burning oil and plastic billowed around its frame. *It's just some animatronic meant to scare the kids,* Justin prayed. Maybe Michelle had set off some trigger. Yet, the intelligent glow in its empty eye sockets withered those hopes.

"Michelle, back away from the water," Cam whispered. "Give me your hand."

The centipede swayed as it scanned the shore. Cam inched to Michelle from one side, Justin from the other.

Before they could grab her, the monster struck.

Air whistled, machinery buzzed, and Michelle sucked in a breath. The centipede scooped her up in its pinchers and whipped its head into the air. She grunted as the monster shook her. Her limbs waved as if they had no bones, even though sickening cracks promised otherwise. Blood splattered the fake grass and sand. Something crunched and squished. Red drool dripped out of her mouth as she bit down hard enough to splinter her teeth, her eyes bulged, a dark liquid leaked from her ears. The creature's legs twitched and scratched at the emptiness. In a blink, it coiled its body and sunk into the mucky pond, the top half of Michelle sticking out.

"Oh shit, oh shit, oh shit!" Cam said.

Michelle waved and screamed, blood bubbling out of her lips as the centipede whipped her around the frothing water, brown and red mixing together. Whenever she passed, Justin willed his body to reach out. The terror radiating out of her red rimmed eyes, the vomit coating her chin and jacket, cursed him for doing nothing. Her horrible whimpering and screams stabbed his heart. Before he could figure out what to do, it dragged her to the center, and they went under.

An uneasy silence settled over the room. For a moment, Justin tried convincing himself a monster hadn't murdered his friend.

"What the actual fuck?" Vince said, his voice shaking.

Cam rushed to the water's edge. The brown pond obscured any sight of the centipede, eddies of crimson danced across the surface. Justin stared, only finding the loss of his friend, the terror of what he'd caused. Aaron raced over, shock enlarging his eyes. Cam sobbed.

"Someone's gotta go get her," Cam said.

"Fuck that, we gotta get the hell out of here!" Aaron said as he wiped his nose. "I loved her too, but that fucking thing might come back. And, well she's probably—"

"No, she can't be dead, she's alive, she's probably just below the surface." Her voice cracked between moans. She marched into the water as she struggled to take her hoodie off. "We can't leave her in there when we are so close, I bet I can get to her I just need to go a little further."

Justin grabbed her and pulled her into him. Memories of Michelle giving him half her lunch every day at school flooded his thoughts. He squeezed Cam before turning her to face him. Tears collected in her eyes. This wasn't supposed to happen. They were supposed to find some cool stuff and remember all the good times they had. No one was supposed to die. "Cam, we can't go in there. What if it attacks you too?"

She strained against him, pushing toward the water. He steeled his body and felt the fight leave her. Cam yelled, "Goddammit!"

Aaron and Vince—surprising all of them—comforted Cam.

"She thought it was so cool I was going on the road with *Fishbone*. Told me I was lucky to get to be a part of the scene like that." Aaron rubbed his nose as he sniffed.

Vince chuckled. "Hell, she could go shot for shot with—"

"Aaron's right, let's get the fuck out of here. God damnit, fuck," Cam said as she turned away from the pond.

"Fuck yeah, sorry Justin, but no way I'm going to hang around with that damn thing in there." Aaron jogged up a hill, whirled toward them and waited.

The words crushed Justin's hopes, even if he knew it was the truth. They truly were never going to come back, especially now.

Justin's shoulders sagged, his voice just above a whisper, "yeah, we can't stay here."

Cam hustled away.

"Fucking shit." Vince glared at them.

Cam stopped. She whipped around, her face red, her teeth bared. "What? What do you want to say? Michelle fucking died, Vince, you fucking asshole."

"Hey, maybe we shouldn't argue next to the murder pond!" Aaron yelled from the hill.

Vince began to speak but Justin put his hand up. "Dude, we can't stay."

Cam left them, her path taking her into the fake trees. She passed Aaron without stopping. He shook his head as he glanced at Justin and Vince. He pointed a thumb in the direction she went and mouthed, *wrong direction*. With a shrug, Aaron ran to the left.

"She was my friend too. But I mean..." Vince said as he found something interesting on the ground.

Wisps of blood floated on the dirty pond. A few bubbles popped along its surface. Anger burned through Justin before it cooled into shame. Vince wanted to stay, wanted to keep pushing through, and he agreed with him. But there's no way they could stay, was there?

"Damn, man, I don't know." He sighed, then shambled after Cam and Aaron. "We should go."

Vince snorted before stomping in the opposite direction.

Track 6

Cresting a hill, Justin spotted Cam testing the opening to a purple cave covered in hearts and stars. "What are you doing?"

"I can't find the door we came in." Her voice husky. "Where's Aaron, I thought he was right behind me?"

"He wasn't sure you went the right way." Justin touched a star. Images of the centipede, of Michelle getting pulled into the pond clouded his mind.

Faint clicks, lapping water, and the whisper of plastic leaves surrounded them. Cam continued to poke the wall, digging her fingers into any crack she found. "I can't believe she's fucking gone. What the hell are we going to say to her parents? Why did we come here?"

Cam lowered her head as she covered her face.

Tears welled up in Justin's eyes. He searched for a way to tell her how sorry he felt, a good enough answer to her question. Nothing came. All he wanted to do was lay down under the fake trees and hide. "I don't remember this... whatever this is."

After a moment she responded, pain deepening her

voice. "It's the *Crag of Sparkle Land*. And I'm pretty positive this is where we came in. I remember walking through those trees over there, and look, there's those fucking shark toys Aaron loved."

He shifted to help her when a shadow darted behind a barricade. "What the fuck?"

"What?"

"I thought I saw something. It was weird. Blue and orange."

"Maybe it was Vince or Aaron," she said as she rushed to the next structure. All he wanted to do was lay down under the fake trees and hide. It took all of his strength to follow her. Cam glanced at him, a question on her face under the black mascara smeared across her cheeks. Did she think he was upset about Michelle? Or did she want him to say it was her fault they came here, and their friend died?

A loud banging followed by Aaron and Vince yelling traveled across the room.

"Maybe they found the way out?" He reached for her. "Let's get out of here. I'll make sure no one else...dies."

She wiped her eyes. "Fuck that. *I'll* make sure none of you die. Y'all are idiots."

The banging continued, Aaron's voice calling them. When they reached the hilltop, their friends near an open door in a rainbow-colored house came into view. As they hustled toward them, water shot out of the pond followed by the centipede.

The monster thrust into the air with a high-pitched squeal. It thrashed about, sending brown water splashing everywhere. Ichor rained down, forming bloody puddles in the fake grass. Cam screamed and covered her head. A torn leg fell into a tree, part of Michelle's plaid mini skirt hooking a branch, an arm knocked over a couple of shark figures, and bits of her torso landed in their path with a splat. The centipede slowed, its red and white mask scanning the room.

"Oh fuck!" Cam said, grabbing Justin, pushing him behind a barricade.

His breath came in ragged gasps as he leaned against the broken pieces of furniture and garbage. They sat listening to the dripping of water, the arrhythmic ticking of clockwork, the patter of what sounded like feet. Twisting, he gaped at a blue and orange shape frolicking amongst the bushes. *God, that thing looks so familiar.* Splatters of blood trickled from the sky. Taking a chance, he snuck a peek around the corner. Aaron and Vince were statues against the rainbow house.

"Shit, what do we do?" he asked.

"We gotta get over to the others," Cam said.

"Do you think it can get out of the water? Vince wasn't—"

"Fuck him, he doesn't know shit." She scratched her head. Then ripped a hunk of wood from the debris. "Only one way to find out."

Cam wound up and tossed the garbage down the hill.

A gurgle and sucking sound followed by the thrashing of legs told them they got its attention. Without checking, they scurried in the opposite direction.

On their left, the centipede scuttled toward some trees. Seeing it out of the water, the glistening segments covered in slimy wet paper and sludge, the jointed legs moving like pistons, the girth of the body a bit taller than him, how there seemed to be no end to its length, sent his mind reeling. *What the fuck did he build this for?* When they were halfway to their friends Cam screamed.

He spun and found her frozen, her focus on the ground. Michelle's decapitated head stared up at her.

Stringy chunks of flesh hung from the torn neck. Thick coagulated blood painted Michelle's mouth, ears, and nose.

Justin rushed to Cam. "We have to go, come on."

She stared at him, tears filling her eyes. "But..."

A terrible screech cut through them.

The centipede twisted; fake trees ripped from the ground. The mask's blank features gave no sign of what it was thinking, if it was thinking, its mandibles clicking in a lazy fashion. It scuttled toward them.

"What the fuck are you guys waiting for, get the fuck over here!" Vince said.

Justin put a hand on Cam's arm. For a moment he weighed the possibility of dragging her. She shuddered, her body drooped, then she jogged ahead of him. The centipede climbed over the hill, smashing the barricade they'd hidden behind. He tempted one last peek at Michelle's head. Brown water leaked down her lips. She cared for him, she never judged him, and now, her dead eyes stared at him. The ground quaked as the monster charged. He backed up a few steps before chasing after Cam, swallowing the pain burning his insides.

Trees whipped by. Toys got caught in his legs. Cam's black hoodie became a shadowy guide. A high-pitched buzz bore into his skull. Aaron screamed for them to hurry. As he cleared the forest and entered a tea party play area, the centipede burst through the woods on his left.

Near the open door, his friends waved their arms like mad. His blood raced. Sweat slickened his back and chest. Behind him came the machine gun drumming of monster legs. A rank odor of burning oil and plastic filled his nostrils.

He kept his eyes focused on Cam and Aaron; Vince was already in the other room.

Pushing his muscles as hard as he could, he didn't notice stepping on something until his ankle twisted. A squeaky voice below him cried for momma. The ground tilted. Gravity flipped his stomach as he fell.

A shadow blotted out the room. Pain shot up his knees and hands when he landed. An insectoid leg pierced the ground next to his head. Sludge dripped onto his back with a plop. He rolled, giving his vision a chance to take in the promised death of the centipede above him.

A hand appeared, the leather wristband dangling from the Black arm a welcome sight. He grabbed it and was pulled away a moment before the monster struck.

"Get your ass moving!" Aaron said, yanking him toward the exit.

They ran. His friends yelled incoherent words. Clock gears ground with a gritty racket. The world quaked. Justin's ankle cried out with each step. All he could do was grit his teeth and keep pushing. A flash of a blue and orange shape danced at the edge of his vision, disappearing into a play structure on the wall. They passed beyond the threshold at the same moment a loud crash came from above.

"Holy shit, what the fuck?" Cam said.

The centipede writhed on the ground, chunks of its shell cracked, amongst the rainbow house's broken pieces. In those shattered bits of plastic, Justin saw his future and wondered if it would have been better if Aaron hadn't saved him from the toy monster.

Vince slammed the door shut.

Track 7

The group collapsed. Behind the door came the grinding of gears, the scraping of legs, the whine of slowing machinery. The walls in the new corridor let off an ambient glow. Justin could only see a few feet beyond where they were standing. It was enough, for now. He needed to focus on his friends. Next to him, Vince leaned against the door. Aaron and Cam stared into space with glassy eyes. Justin took in a deep breath trying to calm his own shaking nerves.

He couldn't believe how fucked this had become. They were supposed to have a great time, and possibly realize college and touring was nowhere near as fun as spending time with him.

Now, he had a dead friend.

Tears welled up and he rested his head against the wall. His traitorous thoughts filled with the excitement of what they had witnessed so far. It skated past visions of Michelle broken body getting whipped around the pond, focusing on the marvel of being in the factory. *Who could have imagined what it'd be like here? Only the toy maker could have created this.* Even with Michelle's decapitated head threatening to come back to his thoughts, he couldn't help but be amazed. Heat flushed his cheeks. *What the fuck is wrong with me?*

"Man, I can't believe she's gone," Aaron said. "Like, what the fuck? She was the only one that pushed me to go on the tour. Hell, she was with me for my first tattoo." He held up his arm to show off a red and black star on his bicep.

Cam sniffed and rubbed her nose. The centipede's scraping and thudding filled the silence.

"What was the point of having that damn thing?" Aaron jerked a thumb toward the Toy Room.

"Maybe Challis had some sort of show set up for them? The water could have fucked up the mechanics or whatever," Justin said.

"Doesn't make me feel any better about what happened. In fact, it makes me more pissed, she died because she was in the wrong place. Fuck that," Vince said.

"Would you be happier to think that thing was alive?" Cam asked.

"I don't know. I didn't think it'd be like this," Vince said.

"Did any of you see that little guy running around?" Aaron asked.

Justin's ears perked up. "Wait, what?"

"No, we are not skipping over what Vince said." Cam stood and stepped toward him. "What did you think would happen? We'd just stumble across a bunch of gold? You dumb sit, there's fucking nothing here."

The centipede's scratching became frantic.

Cam stared at Vince a moment, then turned away, her head down. "This is stupid. Let's just the hell out of here."

Vince's face flushed. His lips curled as he opened his mouth. Before he could speak, Justin punched the wall.

Pain spiked Justin's knuckles. The others stared at him.

Michelle's bloody, mud caked face flashed across his vision, and he knew it was over. He shook his hand, closed his eyes for a moment, and faced his friends. "So, uh, we can't go back in there, right? Probably can only go forward."

"Sure...you alright?" Cam said.

He offered a half smile. "I'm okay."

Vince grumbled as he looked at everything but them.

Aaron nodded. "And maybe stick together. Something tells me we've got a lot more crazy shit coming up."

As if the factory heard him, a row of chandeliers flickered on further down the hall. They all froze, hands up for a fight. Squinting, Justin realized the light fixtures were teddy bear heads, a warm glow emanating from their skulls. The walls were painted in rich golds and reds, bronze cobblestones covering the floor. The hall intersected a path going left and right.

"Aaron's right. Let's just keep on the lookout for anything strange," Justin said, surprising himself at taking the lead.

Cam muttered, "As strange as this hall?"

Their footsteps on the cobblestones echoed along the corridor, almost covering the faint scratching of the centipede. A giddiness wormed its way into Justin's limbs. Part of himself hated this creeping joy at actually being here. It didn't feel right wanting to see what's next so soon after Michelle's death. He knew why the others weren't sharing his excitement but couldn't stop himself from feeling this way. *I'm trying to distract myself, that's all.*

"Do you think this was the only way the kids could go? Or was there more than one way out of there?" He asked.

They kept walking.

"I wouldn't be surprised if Challis gave them a choice. His toys always seemed to be more than what they were,"

Aaron said. "Like, they were sharks, but they were also humans too. It's probably what made his stuff so popular."

A child-like giggle bounced around the hall. The group flattened against the wall. Aaron squawked. Justin stifled a laugh, for as tough as Aaron could be, he scared easily. That wasn't to say it didn't absolutely terrify Justin. No good ever came from an unseen giggle.

"Do you think we should worry about that?" Aaron said.

"Uhm yeah. What the fuck do you think, it's just the wind?" Cam said.

Shadows birthed amorphous shapes of toys and monsters as they waited. Teddy bear lights flickered. The quick breath of Justin's friends replaced the thundering silence. In the distance he caught movement, yet it didn't come toward them. Vince sighed, sauntered into the middle of the space, and peered into the dark. Annoyance slithered through Justin's mind at his friend's impatience. Vince flipped the group off over his shoulder as he stomped down the hall. Aaron snickered before following, cracking his neck and knuckles as if he were going to charge into a mosh pit. Justin and Cam rolled their eyes as they ambled with the others to the end of the hallway and faced their two options.

The right path was swirling shadows, a rank odor of rotten eggs and swampland. On their left, the cobblestones continued, the decadent wall paint melted into twisty candy stripes. More teddy bear chandeliers lit the corridor. The hall ended at a doorway, faint blue light spilling out.

"So, creepy darkness or mysterious door?" Aaron said.

"Fuck the dark. I'd rather go where I can at least see what's coming," Cam said as she began speed walking.

With Cam leading, the others hustled to catch up.

Anticipation bubbled and churned inside Justin like the moments before the main act hit the stage.

"Holy shit. This is insane," she said. "Guess we can officially say this is indeed a factory, though even this is as fucked up as the rest of the place."

When they reached her, they all gazed into the room. Three giant machines with round corners and crooked edges sat in the middle of the space. Bulbous gray pistons with googly eyes peered at them from different spots. Spongy red and blue gears encrusted the device. A wavy conveyor belt—painted like a tongue— stuck out of the first machine. Large cartoon-like eyeballs with spirals and over-sized pupils sat atop each one. Smiling faces had been painted on the walls, with domed lights for eyes. On the opposite side of the room, they saw another opening. The machines watched the group.

"Just when I thought this place couldn't get any crazier, it gives us whatever the hell this is," Vince said.

Aaron tiptoed in. He gazed about, then turned to the others. "Dude, this is wild. It's like that fuckin' cartoon nightmare from *Freddy's Dead.*"

"Hey, there's a door over there." Cam said as she made a beeline for the exit.

Justin and Vince followed her, taking a little longer to stare at the bizarre machines. *As long as we don't touch anything, we should be fine.* The thought barely finished forming in Justin's head when he noticed Aaron picking up what looked like a dead raccoon.

"What the fuck? Don't touch anything, man," Justin said.

"Assholes, let's go," Cam said.

"But, look at this, it's an empty stuffed animal. So weird," he said, holding up the floppy skin. He pointed to a rack full of cardboard boxes near the exit wall, a pile of skins on the floor.

"You think that's weird, check this out," Vince said. He stood next to a pit near the middle machine.

"We really don't have time for this. Or did you forget about Michelle dying?" Cam asked.

Justin's spirits dropped. He knew she was right. They needed to keep moving. Swallowing the fear of speaking up, as well as disappointing the others, he joined Cam. "Guys Cam's right. I think we should probably get out of here."

"Fuck." Aaron tossed one of the empty skins down. "Sorry, this is just fucking weird and shit. But, yeah, I get it."

Aaron dragged a finger along one of the conveyor belts, his wrist band rubbing against the rubber, as he shuffled over to the others.

The three of them glanced at Vince, who continued to study the room.

"Vince, get your ass moving, come on," Cam said.

"Do you think this still works?" Vince asked as he sauntered past the machines.

"Who gives a shit?" Cam said.

"It'd probably try to turn us into bears, if it did." Aaron said. "Fucking psycho place."

Justin's heart became lead and sunk into his stomach. This was really over. He hated that he held on to a glimmer of hope. Did it make him a terrible person? He knew the answer and cursed himself. The best he could do now was get them out and pray they would forgive him.

Cam pushed Aaron on her way to the door. She stopped mid stride.

"Uh, did you all hear that?"

"What?" Vince sidled up to her and cocked his head. "I don't hear anything."

"I thought I heard giggling again."

"Maybe it's just an echo in your head or something, you know?" Aaron said.

"Yeah, there's nothing out there." Vince brushed past Cam. Before he could leave, a child-sized, light pink hand reached out from the darkness. "Oh fuck!"

Track 8

Justin's nerves crackled. Vince never freaked out, never jumped when the cops spotlighted the underpass he spent time under, never pissed himself when a crackhead pulled a knife on him. *What the fuck could it be?* Something told Justin not to look. He shifted to peek past his friend's shoulder. A petite, shiny face with sparkling, dead eyes, rosy cheeks, and pouting mouth peered from the dark.

He wished he'd listened to himself and didn't look.

The doll waddled into the entrance. Bulgy legs poked out of a cornflower blue checked dress. Shoulder length brown hair barely moved as it came at them. Light bounced off its squeaky black shoes. Goosebumps prickled Justin's skin as the figure ambled forward. Its arms reached for someone to pick it up. He didn't notice any strings, any human hands controlling it. He couldn't remember if Challis Toys ever promoted a walking doll. The face never changed from its innocence. Yet that mask of pureness haunted him more than any scary monster ever could.

Aaron shuffled away from the door while doing the sign

of the cross. A slight waver softened his voice, "just kick the fucking thing."

The doll continued its duck walk toward Justin, Cam, and Vince. Aaron circled behind them to Justin's left and closer to the first machine. When it reached hugging distance, it raised its arms. The three took a big step back. The doll giggled and followed. Vince cursed. The distance between them and the door increased. Sweat stung Justin's eyes. As he wiped it away, he swore he saw another shadow dance into the room, sneaking around the boxes near an oversized red button on the wall. Each step backwards led them closer to the pit of fluff. Before they'd fall in, he told himself he'd do something.

Besides, what could one doll do?

"You fucking pansies." Confidence filled Aaron's voice as he sprinted at the doll. He pulled back his leg like he was a kicker for a football team. The baby doll launched itself into the air and attached itself to his pants.

"Holy shit, what the fuck?" He shook his leg as he danced around. "It's biting me or something!"

"Wait, stop moving," Cam said as she rushed toward him.

A cartoonish boing cut through the tension. Flashing lights flickered on as a distorted cheery voice filled the room: "Hey hey, kids! Feed me your special baby and watch me give it life!"

A clunking, grinding, metal rhythm started as the machines began running.

"What the hell is going on?" Vince said as he hugged himself and squatted, his gaze bouncing around the room.

Aaron continued to fight with the doll. "It really fucking hurts."

Cam reached out to help Aaron, all the color drained from her face. "Give me one second."

He kept bouncing, getting closer and closer to the moving conveyor belt. Justin saw where this was going if they didn't stop him. A grimace scrunched up Aaron's face. Whatever held Justin back let go and he sprinted toward his friend. Fear spiked his lungs and clenched his heart. Moments before he could touch Aaron's hoodie, his friend lost his footing.

In slow motion he toppled onto the conveyor belt.

If Justin didn't know any better, he'd have thought the machine was alive and hungry because as soon as Aaron hit the tongue-colored belt it sped up. Robotic arms swung out of the machine at Aaron, one smacking him on the head with a wet crunch. They could practically watch the stars dancing in his eyes as his limbs twitched. Justin tried grabbing Aaron, but another metal arm whipped around, knocking him on his ass. Vince helped him up, his eyes wild, his mouth a trembling line as he muttered *fucking dolls*. Cam jumped and grabbed Aaron's doll-free leg. He bounced on the belt, but she stopped him from being pulled into the machine.

"Aaron, come on you gotta roll over." Cam glared at Vince and Justin. "Guys!"

Vince didn't move, his eyes glued to the doll. "Why is it moving? Why is it alive? It can't do that."

Justin shook his head, he didn't have time to figure out Vince's problem, and rushed in to help.

The doll released Aaron and crawled toward Cam, *momma* coming from its unmoving lips. Cam gasped, her fingers loosening on Aaron's pants. One of the machine's spindly metal arms spun, grazing the air next to her head.

She jerked back, losing her grip on Aaron. Justin ducked another swinging part and clasped Aaron's hand.

"I got you," Justin said. His friend's head thrummed against the belt's slats, leaving traces of blood behind.

Cam screamed as the doll pulled at her face, its baby voice pleading with her. Curses, growls, and pain spewed from her mouth. The toy gripped Cam's cheeks tighter as she yanked at its body. Red streaks tore jagged lines in the flesh under the doll's chubby fingers.

"Fuck!" Vince's voice rose above the grinding machinery. Revulsion curled his lips as he grabbed its plastic arms. His eyes twitched while he held it as far from his body as he could. Vince hurled the doll across the room. It cried for momma as it crashed into the boxes of skins. He howled before chasing the toy.

Frantic energy coursed through Justin as he held onto Aaron. "We got you."

The veins in Justin's hands bulged as he fought against the torrent of machinery. His muscles tremored and threatened to quit. More and more of Aaron's body hung off the belt, encouraging Justin to pull harder.

"Almost the—" he felt Aaron's body go rigid before being jerked forward. Staring, he noticed Aaron's leather wristband, caught in a slat. He struggled to keep his grip. The machine won the tug of war and yanked Aaron into the plexiglass box.

All they could do was watch.

Aaron's eyes flickered open as two arms with scalpel fingers ripped open his hoodie and sliced into his chest. Beads of scarlet appeared before becoming a torrent pouring out of his skin. A pair of new arms with delicate metal claws stretched open his torso with a sick squelch. The fresh opening revealed his ribcage, the frantic throbbing of organs, crimson pools flooding everything. Their friend screamed and squirmed. Blood splattered against the plexiglass. Cam held a hand to her mouth, tears in her eyes.

"That part there, maybe we can still save him!" Justin sprinted toward the uncovered section of the conveyor belt between the first and second machine.

The track clicked as it carried Aaron's body into the open. He writhed and moaned, the sound breaking Justin's heart. A rain of blood dripped from the belt onto the floor. With one hand out, Justin touched his friend's shoe before Aaron was sucked in.

The eyes at the top of the boxy contraption spun faster and faster. A claw dug into the pit and pulled out a hefty load of fluffy white cotton. The machine let out a static filled sound of glee. Cam joined Justin. He wanted to leave, to run away. He grabbed her hand and squeezed. Their jaws dropped as another robotic limb shoved a square funnel into Aaron's chest, blood and flesh squirting every-where. The loud crack of his ribs sounded like someone slamming through plywood. His arms and legs jerked. A trickle of ichor slipped down his lips. He blinked at them. Cam pounded on the glass.

"Where the fuck is Vince?" Justin scanned the room and spotted his friend near the shelving unit, stomping the doll. The red button within arm's reach. Justin prayed it was an emergency stop button. "Vince, turn the goddamn machine off!"

The crane full of cotton positioned itself above the funnel. The claw opened, a distorted belch coming from hidden speakers, and dumped its load. Bits of fluff piled on top. A heavy metal rod shoved the cotton into Aaron's body, flinging some into the air. Errant tufts landed on his face and stuck to his tears and blood. It forced more down. His chest and stomach bulged. The pole raised and came down again, pushing deeper into the funnel. His skin stretched until jagged, dark red tears appeared. Once the funnel had fully been cleared it was lifted out of his body. Cotton and gore clung to Aaron's shirt and chest. He coughed and some fluffy material puffed out of his mouth, floated out of the wound. A mound of stuffing sat on his open chest, melting in his viscera.

Helplessness weighed Justin down, horror scuttled over his nerves.

Cam let out a cry: "Goddammit, Vince, we have to stop this."

She ran toward the button. Justin stayed, unable to leave Aaron alone.

More arms appeared, this time with a thick needle and black thread. With the precision only a machine can have, it slid the sharp point through Aaron's skin with a slight pop and hiss. Bits of gore clung to the string. Justin saw his friend as he did at school, proudly sporting a *Mustard Plug* hoodie and getting in a fight with some rednecks because "Black kids should only listen to rap." Cotton snuck out between the stitches like dark red slugs. The metal arm gave one final tug, snapping the thread. A puckered wound covered the length of his torso.

The moment it finished, Justin came to his senses. "Shit, fuck, motherfucker! Someone turn this fucking thing off!"

He tore his gaze away from his friend and directed it to the others. Vince shuddered, his head in his hands. Cam slammed boxes aside, cursing Vince and Challis. She had her hand up when she squawked and yanked her arm back. "Something swiped at me."

The machine screeched. A jaunty tune that could have

been from a children's show, played in time with the conveyor belt whipping Aaron into the last station.

"Oh my god, what now?" Justin said as he followed his friend's body.

Out of the corner of his eye he saw Cam kicking at the shadows while punching the button at the same time.

Nothing stopped.

Vince appeared to wake from his stupor and dived at the thing attacking Cam.

"Why won't this fucking work?" she yelled as she bashed the controller.

Aaron groaned, one of his fingers wiggling toward Justin. The music continued to play.

Within the metal, gears, and plexiglass destination, spindly arms ending in metal bats slammed against the belt with heavy thuds.

"Oh god no." Justin punched the window, tears streaking his cheeks. Witnessing Michelle's death was too much, but that had gone by fast.

But this?

This kept fucking going.

"We can't stay here; we gotta leave." He backed away from the machine.

Cam shuffled to Justin's side, her body deflating at the sight of the metal bats. Vince appeared next to them, took one look and whispered *fuck*. The three shambled backwards, unable to stop themselves from watching.

The belt guided Aaron deeper into the machine. The clubs were up in the air. He put a crimson hand on the plexiglass.

"Now let's get your teddy bear all fluffy for your magical nights snuggling in bed!" a goofy cartoon-like voice announced.

The clubs came down.

They weren't fast enough to finish Aaron off. The smacks filled the room, tattooing themselves onto Justin's brain. Syrupy blood squirted from wounds, mouth, ears, nose, sticking to Aaron and machinery. A bat smashed into his skull, popping out an eye. Another smack shattered his teeth. Bones cracked, arms and legs bent into unnatural positions. Each hit sent out a flurry of cotton. Aaron groaned for a while. Then he was silent.

When the process finished, the conveyor belt dumped Aaron's body into a box. The cardboard tore as he flopped to the floor.

Time stretched and twisted its claws in, so they'd never forget this image of his stuffed corpse.

Cam broke free of Vince and Justin, the toy version of her friend, and hustled out of the room. Vince wobbled a few feet away and vomited. He wiped his mouth, before stumbling behind Cam, punching the wall on his way out. Justin stood alone with his shredded hopes.

Lost in a fog, Justin tore his attention away from his friend's body. This was his fault. There was nothing he could say or do to bring them back, to make it better for Cam and Vince, for Aaron or Michelle's parents. What's the point in him ever leaving here? If they can even leave. The concept seemed less likely with each passing minute. He dragged his feet to the exit. Motion pulled him to the present when his friends—fear plastered on their faces— sprinted past the door.

Track 9

A torrent of thoughts whipped through him as he stared at the door. His friends' footfalls slapped down the hall. *Maybe they found a way out?* Though, he wondered if they were trying to ditch him. He couldn't blame them. Because of him, their friends were dead. Should he try to follow? What was waiting for him out there? A life without his closest people. The constant ache reminding him that he'd killed two of them and drove the others away. Shaking his head, he shuffled to the doorway, hoping maybe he could help them get out, do one thing right by them.

Something nagged him, so he glanced around. A gaggle of frilly dressed porcelain dolls waddled toward him.

He chased after his friends.

Sounds of padding feet and cries for momma followed him. The cobblestones of the previous hall had morphed into lush Oriental rugs. Candelabras replaced the glass teddy bear chandeliers. Dingy paintings of toys and children dotted the walls above wooden chair rails and paneling. Long gouges and burn marks appeared in random places along the hall. Pieces of broken glass and printer paper collected on the floor. Despite the dolls being behind him, he couldn't help himself from daydreaming about what it'd have been like to be here every day.

Ahead, Cam and Vince disappeared around a corner. He rode the wave of possible annihilation at the tiny porcelain hands of the dolls as he careened down the hall, passing doors and intersections, after his friends. He could track the sweat dripping down the back of Vince's neck, and lock breathing patterns with Cam's puffing. *Fuck, they're slowing down.* A peek over his shoulder, gave him the perfect view of the dolls' shining eyes, the slight cracks in their clear faces. Grimacing, he focused on catching up.

"Where are we going?" his voice came out in gasps.

Vince said, "Finding. A. Place. To. Hide."

They came to an intersection and Vince led them to the right. Crooked doors painted in neon reds and blues with cartoonish, round doorknobs lined the hall.

"Pick one!" Justin yelled. Cam was already opening a random door and entering, Vince behind her. Justin dived in, and the others slammed the door shut.

After a moment face down on a dark hardwood floor, Justin pushed himself up. Warm buttery light bathed the room. From some corner came a hush that reminded Justin of waiting at the doctor's office. Cam sat hunched against a desk with her knees covering her face. Her sobbing sliced Justin's heart like a razor. A few darkened brass lamps were sprinkled throughout, sitting on end tables and workbenches near the edges of the room. An oily aroma overpowered a faint moldy odor. Huge banners featuring Challis standing next to baby dolls, robotic warriors, and stuffed monsters adorned the walls.

The sight of the dolls chilled him. He whirled and

rushed to the door. The ornate handle didn't have a lock, just an otherworldly face with an obscene pointed nose and puffy cheeks. A quick scan and he found a wingback chair in a corner. Dragging it over, he propped it in front of the door.

"Goddamn, do you know what—" Vince began to say before Justin put a finger to his mouth.

They listened to the chorus of *mommas* coming from the other side. Their focus zeroed in on the chair. Justin prayed the combined strength of the dolls wouldn't be enough to open the door. Out of all the ways he assumed he'd die; this wasn't even on the list. Shadows passed by the crack under the door. Justin's muscles tensed. A slight tap against the wood became a death knell.

"Momma?"

Cam scooted to the side of the door. Vince appeared next to Justin. A grim acceptance lined their faces.

After a stomach-churning moment, the dolls moved on.

The group released a collective breath. Cam slid down to the floor; her eyes glazed over. Vince went right back to the desk.

"As I was saying, I'm pretty positive we found Challis' office! You know what this fucking means, right?" He held his arms up. "We hit the fucking jackpot. Just need to find the bastard's safe and we're golden."

Despite the terror and helplessness of losing two friends, hope blossomed in Justin's chest. The massive desk covered in dusty papers and blueprints, workbenches filled with half-finished projects, glass cases highlighting old toys, they were in the epicenter of Challis' domain. If there really was a safe, it had to be here. Was there a chance the death of his friends could be made right by what they found? Probably not. But it could ease the pain. At least, he hoped.

"Really? That's what you're thinking about right now? Michelle and Aaron just fucking died." Cam stood and slammed her fist into a case. Clockwork toys rattled; a toy ninja fell over. "You really are the worst fucking person."

Vince kicked the desk. His eyes were bloodshot, snot clung to his upper lip, as he glared at them. Sorrow crusted his voice. "No. That's not all that I care about. They were my friends too. Aaron helped me out of more jams than either of you know about. Michelle always had a way to make me laugh. So, fuck you for thinking that.

"I just don't want their fucking horrifying way of dying to be pointless. I want to fucking take all the money fucking Challis has. I want to find his fucking corpse and beat the bloody shit out of it. I want to stuff fucking cotton up his goddamn ass until it comes out of his fucking shit-stained mouth. I want to feed his twitching body to a bunch of fucking bugs."

Challis' grin glared down at them from the banners. Toys observed from their glass cages. Cam and Vince stared each other down. Justin's body locked. How could he let his last two friends hate each other? Cam would never come back if he sided with Vince. As much as the money would be nice, he needed her friendship in his life more. Frustration, confusion, and depression boiled inside him until he became helpless.

The office's artifacts allowed him a moment to avoid their fight. The scuffed-up work benches where Challis had built his first toys were like altars used by gods. Clockwork gears, tools, metal molds, and plastic limbs made him think of the building blocks of life. If it weren't for the murderous energy permeating the factory, Justin would want to stay within this magical world forever.

The magic crashed down as his traitorous mind told him he was selfish.

The word flashed through his mind. If he wasn't so stupid and focused on himself, he would have known they weren't really leaving him. They were going to college, going on tour. None of that meant they weren't coming back. And what did it matter if they had fun while gone? That wouldn't have erased what the group had together. They had a bond, and nothing would have broken that.

Except for death.

"I think we should leave. Tell their parents what happened. I'll take the blame. It was my fault you all came here. I wanted you all to think you'd never have as much fun without me. I'm sorry. For everything," Justin said.

Cam wrapped Justin in her arms. Vince opened his mouth then turned away.

"Dude, we could have said no. It's definitely not your fault this place is fucked up. You didn't kill them," Cam said.

"But..."

"Listen, we weren't going to leave you all alone. Michelle..." Cam blinked a few tears away. "We were going to ask if you wanted to come up north with us. We got an old house, like one of the student ghetto houses down here, so there's space in the attic."

Justin's whole world dropped out from under him. *They wanted to take me?* He couldn't breathe. If he had chilled out and stopped being so crazy, none of this would have happened. Hate grew knives and broken glass in his throat. Why did he have to always assume the world was dealing him a shit sandwich?

Vince grabbed cabinets and tables, knocking them to the floor with a crash. He picked up a wrench and slammed it into a wall, tearing a jagged hole into a banner. "It has to be fucking here! Where the fuck is your money, you bastard!"

Something snapped in Justin. For himself, for his friends, he had to do better. Starting now. "Vince, come on man, it's pointless, we're not going to find shit."

"No way, it's here. My buddy knew a guy that knew a guy that knew a security guard here that said they are getting paid in cash, at the front gate. Some dude would come down from the factory. It's here somewhere." Vince continued to tear the place apart.

Justin glanced at Cam. A spark glinted in her eyes. They all thought he was bullshitting them anytime he brought the place up. This information wasn't much, a mortgage company could be sending someone here to make sure the guards were doing their job. He could be lying.

Or it could be here.

"Alright, let's look for like ten minutes and then get the fuck out of here," Justin said. If they found it, they could use it to offset funeral costs, or cover Michelle's half of the rent for Cam, or do anything that might alleviate the terrible mistake of coming here.

Track 10

Shredded banners hung from the walls. Paper, broken toys, shattered tables littered the floor. An upended bookshelf leaned against a cracked glass case. Empty desk drawers were scattered in a corner. Vince crawled under a workbench while Cam tossed books over her shoulder. Bits of garbage clung to Justin's hoodie, scratches crisscrossed his hands, his mind hollow.

It's not here. He hung his head as he stared at a rectangular cabinet that reminded him of an aquarium he'd seen holding a couple of ball pythons at Willow Oaks Mall once, though this was probably twice as big. Exhaustion whispered in his ear to give up. *It'll be the last thing I check.* Ornate wood panels concealed the bottom two thirds with a dusty glass case on top. Within, filthy red moth-eaten curtains hung along each side. A dull black button stuck out of the center of the front panel. Strange energy emanated off the object that sent goosebumps up and down his arms.

Depression and fear told him to walk away, there wasn't going to be any money in there. Yet, he took a step forward, saw himself from outside as he kneeled, putting his head level with the container, and traced a finger around the button. *What could it hurt?* A million answers came to mind. None of them stopped him.

It felt like sand filled his mouth as he spied on the others to make sure they didn't see him.

He pressed the button.

Deep within the cabinet, clockwork ticked like a heart stuttering to life. The curtain flapped before sliding open to reveal a miniature stage. Dollhouse-sized bulbs along the bottom flickered to life, plastering the scene with harsh yellow light. A sheet of plastic molded to look like brick, with thin oblong holes tracing paths across it, made up the floor. The background had two doorways on the left and right, miniature hinges in the middle, and a crude interpretation of the factory painted on it. Justin's chest thundered, his eyes watered. An action figure-sized tin Challis appeared in the right door. His movements were jerky as he repeatedly lifted his hat from his round head. The factory owner had a skinny metal pole attached to a spot between his legs down to one of the paths. It guided him to center stage. Challis spun back and forth before bending and shaking his head in what Justin thought was sadness, despite the black smile and violet eyes on his face. After a moment, the figure slid back into the door. A loud thunk came from the cabinet as one half of the background flipped like a page in a book, revealing a new scene.

Large, jagged leaves hung from curly trees, unfamiliar yellow and brown, round fruits stuck out of branches painted on the backdrop. Shadows clung to the ground, insectoid legs appeared behind trunks, dark shapes peered from the jungle's depths. Justin's muscles quivered when he saw a group of impish tin creatures glide out of the left door as Challis came from the right. The poles stuck up their asses bounced them in a scampering motion. Blue skin covered their skeletal frames. Arms with plate-sized hands hung to the ground. They had pointed noses and almond shaped eyes under wild orange hair. At first, he thought of *Tool*'s music videos and their unsettling Claymation, then a new memory bubbled up and his insides solidified. *I've seen these fuckers here!* The imps met Challis at the middle of the stage. The leader and the factory owner hopped in front of each other. Challis reached out and bumped a round hand against the creature's hand. All the characters swiveled on their sticks and were shuttled into the background.

His scalp crawled, a loud hush filled his ears, and his nerves crackled when the scene changed to a new version of the factory. A swirling green and purple portal had been painted around a door. Two-dimensional toys missing their top halves popped out of the stage. Challis glided to each plaything and guided the imps from the portal into the toys. Each time an imp entered one, the top appeared and completed the object. A cut-out picture of a child drawn in a 1950's children's book style would slide up from a trap door and drag the imp-filled toy back under the stage. The process continued over and over until Justin's head spun.

He touched the Challis button on his hoodie, the seal that promised the toy was made with magic. Was he trying to say the imps were the magic? The scene continued to play. He watched, flashing back to every glimpse of the blue and orange creatures he'd seen in the factory. He saw the broken toys spread throughout the Toy Room and the lobby. A headache pulsed at his temples as he attempted comprehending what it all meant.

More imps popped out of the stage, outnumbering the toys, filling the case. The tin Challis spun in place, bumping into the creatures, his arms out in front of him. He backed toward the door, the imps following him. The curtain closed before Challis could escape.

Justin leaned back on his knees, waiting for his heart to slow.

"What the fuck? Nothing!" Vince said.

"Shit!" Justin fell on his ass, surprised from his friend's outburst. Vince stood in front of the desk rubbing his cheek, Cam near a bookcase.

"All I found were these weird books and a bunch of stupid shit that isn't money or a safe." Cam held up two tattered hardcovers, the titles missing. "I think your security dudes lied."

Justin wondered if he should show them the machine, then shuddered at the idea of watching it again, as he joined them.

"What's the book? Could be worth something," Vince said as he sidled up to Cam.

"Fuck if I know." Cam flipped through the pages.

Bizarre circles with lines crossed through them, pentagrams that belonged on a *Cannibal Corpse* CD, and black inked symbols ran across the pages. There were diagrams of an upside-down triangle with a circle in the middle. Lines went from the triangle to five boxy shapes. When they got to a page with the imps on it, Justin's skin crawled.

"Didn't one of you see blue people like this in the toy room?" Cam said as she glanced at them.

"I don't know, maybe," Justin spit the words out hoping they wouldn't notice. "It fucking sucks, but it's past time to get the hell out of here." Justin kicked a broken table. If he could at least get them out of the factory, he'd be happy he did something right by them. His new goal in life would be to make it up to them and memory of Aaron and Michelle.

Cam put the books down. "Finally. But, uh, how?"

"I've been thinking about it," Justin said, moving toward the door. "We have to go back the way we came. It's the only definite way we know of that has an exit. I'm pretty positive I remember how we got here."

The others stared at him, their eyebrows crawling up on their foreheads.

"Whoa, look at you!" Cam said. "Usually, your plan is to just look for the other dudes with mohawks and safety pins and follow them. Remember how long it took us to find The Ice Pick? Didn't think we were going to be able to see *The Vandals* at all that night."

"Yeah, well, this is a bit different," he chuckled. "Fuck, that was a great show too."

Justin went to a side table. With a swift kick, he removed a table leg. "I think if we have a weapon, we can knock those fucking dolls out of our way."

Cam found a length of chain hanging on a workbench. Vince wandered to the back and grabbed the wrench he had used earlier. When they were ready, they lined up next to the door. Justin studied his friends. Dust, sweat, and tears streaked their faces. They gripped their weapons tight. Slight curls turned up the corners of their mouths. If this was the last night he'd be with them, at least they could have some fun destroying something for the sake of those they lost.

Track 11

Not a single doll waited for them in the hall. A faint hum hung in the air. Massive faces of screaming children were painted on the walls. Within each stretched mouth, a door waiting to be opened. As they retraced their steps toward the Toy Room, Justin hated how the eyes watched them.

"This is fucking creepy," Cam said.

"Like what the fuck?" Justin said.

"I don't get it. No way the kids would have enjoyed this." Cam touched a face. "It's like Challis was messing with people, trying to freak them out."

"Yeah. This whole thing is not what I imagined when I was I kid. It's like a fucked up haunted house." Justin spun and walked backwards. "Do you remember passing these faces?"

"I..." Vince glanced around. "No. But, maybe I was too focused on the fucking dolls. There's an intersection up ahead, maybe that'll give us an idea."

They hustled until they faced five possible options.

"Did we go the wrong way?" Cam said.

The path they were on continued ahead, more faces going toward the darkness. The left and right halls that would be the top of a Y had moving spotlights, polka dots on the walls. Perpendicular to their location, the halls resembled round tunnels, lines of Christmas lights swirling around the curved walls. The ornate hallway Justin remembered running through was gone.

"Should we go back? Maybe we missed a door or path?" Cam said.

"I honestly don't remember," Justin said. Panic whispered in his ears. He focused on mentally mapping the turns they had made.

"I think that's the way." He pointed towards the right, down the tunnel with Christmas lights. "At least that seems like the general direction we came in."

Cam nodded at Justin. Pride blossomed in his chest despite the new feeling of taking charge.

"Are you sure?" Vince said.

"Well, I guess it's as good as any, right? But, I'm pretty positive we didn't take too many turns, so like, this should skip the hall with the stuffed animal machine and Aaron's..."

Cam waved the thought away. "Works for me. Let's get the fuck out of here."

Slumped shoulders and shuffling feet led them down the tunnel of red and green twinkling lights.

"Hey, do you smell that?" Cam asked.

The question seemed to bring about the scent of flowers, cooking meat, and gasoline.

"Oh shit!" Vince said.

The crew picked up their pace. In the distance, a dark

violet rectangle floated. The faint chirp of crickets called to Justin. Hope drummed on his heart.

Cam gasped when they reached a tall window at the end of the hall.

"Fucking yes!" Vince said. "Let's get the fuck out of here!"

Below them were a line of houses, front porch lights, small as lightning bugs, marked the suburban streets. Further out, they could spot the town. Above, the moon glowed bone white along with twinkling stars.

"Wait, did we climb stairs or something? I don't remember being this high or houses being this close to the factory," Vince said.

"Maybe we didn't notice a rise in the floor. But, we're at a window, a way out!" Justin said. He didn't mention the stale air or lack of any moving headlights.

Sticking his head out, he counted the windows on the factory wall and guessed they were fifty feet or so up. *Not going to be able to jump.* To his right, he spotted a few pipes within reach—if he stretched—attached to the building.

"I'm going to climb down. You guys stay here." He pointed outside. "It should be fine, but I'd rather be the one to test it. If I...don't make it, I'm really sorry for bringing you all here."

Vince shook his head while looking out the window. Cam screwed up her mouth as she continued studying Justin and the outside.

"Fuck, that's a long way down. I don't know about this," she said as she laid a hand on his back.

"It's okay." He dropped his weapon and leaned out the window.

Vertigo swirled the outside world. Reaching out, he

gripped the gritty pipe and shook. It didn't budge. Holding on, he asked Vince for a boost. His friend studied him, exhaled, then helped. A lump formed in Justin's throat as he waited for the drainpipe to tell him if it could handle his full weight. When it didn't break, he said a short prayer and scooted down.

After a few minutes, his muscles tremoring and begging to stop, he glanced down. Crickets chirped. The air hung heavy on his frame. He had made good progress, but the ground still seemed so far away. Nerves spiked his stomach.

The pipe vibrated, metal groaned, something pinged and scuttered, someone cried out. Before he could put it all together, the pipe bent, and he was falling.

Air rushed by. He waited for his life to replay before his eyes. All that came were images of smashing to the ground, of his body liquifying, bones shattering. Above him were the shrinking faces of Cam and Vince, their arms reaching. He hated he'd gotten them close to a way out and broke the pipe. If he could go back through time, he would remove the pain of them leaving, he'd remove ever suggesting coming here. He'd trade his life for his friends.

Justin hit the ground.

Every part of him cried out in pain. Stars pogoed before his eyes, a coppery sting sat on his tongue. But he wasn't dead. Maybe it was going to take longer, his internal organs leaking, his brain melting into mush. He closed his eyes. His last thoughts conjured Cam's voice, speaking to him in an unintelligible language. Death tortured him by taking its sweet time to claim him. His back itched. Why did he hate that his friends were moving on? He should have been happy for them. Instead of guilting them, he should have used their example as inspiration. He grew angry for coming to these thoughts now, as he was dying.

"Hey! Are you alright?" Cam said.

If he wasn't positive about dying, he would have answered.

"Dude, I don't think you fell that far," Vince said.

What is he talking about? He basically swan dived fifty feet. He wasn't going to let death tease him by speaking with their voices.

There was a thud, a grunt, someone touched him. Maybe angels really existed?

"Justin, are you okay? Where does it hurt?" The angel sounded like Vince.

"I'm dead. I fell like twenty stories. It hurts everywhere."

"Fuck, dude, it was more like ten feet."

"Then I'm in hell."

Another pair of hands searched his chest. "Nothing seems to be broken. Stop being a fucking pussy. Remember that time I stage dived off *The Suicide Machines'* amp at that bar in Hamtramck? No one caught me and I landed on the floor? That was further than this."

Justin couldn't help but laugh. The intense pain he expected was nothing more than throbbing ribs. "Oh god, don't make me laugh, Cam. You fucking didn't even check when you jumped, you asshole."

Deciding to try, he opened his eyes. Cam and Vince were above him, smirking. Beyond them, the stars twinkled in the night sky. The factory loomed on his right, each of its windows triangular shaped with the bigger part on top. A dull ache squelched around in his skull. Taking it slow, he pushed himself onto his elbows. Beyond Cam he could make out the houses. They appeared smaller than they should. He didn't see or hear any movement, except the crickets. At first, he thought about blaming the fall for his vision issues. Then, it dawned on him that Vince might be right.

"God, that fucking hurt," Justin said.

"Not as much as what I'm going to tell you," Cam said.

"That we haven't left the factory at all?"

"Yep."

Track 12

The world spun a few times as Justin stood, his back wailing in pain. He stared up at the window they had come from. Heat warmed his cheeks as he saw how close it was.

"So, what the fuck is all of this?" He motioned toward the houses.

"I have no idea," Cam said as she got off the ground to stand next to Justin.

"Damn this is a fucking tease!" Vince said.

"It's so weird. There's gotta be a door somewhere, right?" Justin said.

"Yeah, I don't think we got in here the way Challis expected," Vince said with a laugh.

"What is this room?" Cam walked ahead, growing taller with each step until she towered over the houses nearby. "Is it like a fucking model?"

"Shit, I don't even know anymore. Let's just find a way the hell out," Justin said.

The three followed a road about the width of Justin's

feet. Hills and trees coated the floor. It only took a couple of steps to start walking amongst the structures. Rooftops of buildings reached his thighs. They had to walk single file, Vince leading and Cam taking the rear. There were porches and driveways, swing sets and garages, streetlights, and mailboxes. It appeared so realistic he couldn't help but imagine them as giants smashing through a town. After each step they took, house lights went out, and Justin swore he could hear tiny screams. An uneasy feeling washed over him, and he urged the others to move faster.

The air grew electric, the crickets quieted. Justin's heart stopped. Bright spotlights flicked on, scanning the air until they landed on the three of them.

"Go!" he said.

A tinny siren groaned and whined. The hairs on Justin's arms bristled. He tried moving faster, but the houses and tight streets forced them to shuffle in a line. From behind came the thump of marching, squeaky cries and orders being barked.

"Shit, something's coming!" Cam said.

Justin and Vince turned and found her facing away from them. A battalion of soldier action figures carrying plastic guns filled the streets beyond Cam. Black clad ninjas holding brown swords sprinted across rooftops. The toys' faces were stuck in grimaces, making their battle cries confusing and disturbing. Tanks, and alien vehicles with too many wheels and too many guns followed the army.

"Holy shit, it's the GUN Brigade!" Vince said. "I totally had some of them when I was a kid."

"Of course you did," Cam said.

"What? They were rad. All their crazy stories, the way they had these super powerful guns that shot little darts. Sucked that some stupid kid shot his eye out."

They stood mesmerized as the toys got into formation. The tap of plastic boots marching in sync created a stereo effect. Reinforcements joined the army until they filled the streets.

"Come on," Justin said. *Are there imps in them? Can they get that small?*

The group backed up a few steps when the action figures fired.

Tiny pops filled the room. Justin questioned if there'd actually be bullets, then chided himself, of course there would be. Cam waved her arms in front of her face as she let out annoyed grunts.

"Cam, you okay?" Justin said.

"Yeah. More annoyed than anything." She stayed in place, staring down the soldiers.

"Cool. I think we're pretty close to the other side of the room." Justin craned his neck and spotted Vince's silhouette against the fake night sky, his gaze at something above him on the wall. "Vince, start searching for a way out!"

He attempted pulling Cam away. She shrugged him off.

"I'm really sick of this shit." She stomped toward the armies. Each footfall sent the soldiers stumbling or toppling over. A few broke ranks and ran. Panicked screams squeaked out from houses. Doors opened and blocky people sprinted for safety. The cries grew louder, the words "monster," "beast," and "unnatural" taking shape. Cam slowed, tracking frightened toys running from her.

"Cam, let's go," Justin said.

"No! Why are they screaming at me? I'm not the monster. They are." She grabbed a small blocky girl in a pink shirt with brown plastic hair, exaggerated eyelashes painted over brown dot eyes. "You're the fucking monsters!

You're nothing but fucking toys! You are not supposed to be alive!"

The girl wiggled its arms, a piercing wail coming from unmoving lips. Some of the soldiers regrouped near the tanks. Others sprinted into houses or cowered.

Worry tattooed a drum beat on Justin's brain. Memories of those early days during junior year at school, the slurs and insults hurled at Cam burned in his head.

"Cam..." he said.

She bellowed.

He'd heard Cam scream at assholes, he'd heard her sadness when their music couldn't capture her feelings, he'd heard her argue with her mom. He'd never heard this strange, unhinged timbre in her voice.

"I am not the fucking monster!" Cam wound back her arm, and whipped it around, pitching the figure into the distance.

The toys went silent. They tracked their fellow toy as it sailed through the air. It hit the wall barely making a sound.

Cam's sobs filled the room.

Mental alarms blasted in Justin's head. He whispered, "Cam, it's okay. You are not a monster. But now's our chance to get out of here."

Faster than he expected, army toys with articulated limbs and action grips scuttled up her pants. Others squeezed into the spaces between her boots and jeans. She kicked and danced, releasing a deep guttural noise. She tried brushing them off. Some of the toys fell, only to be replaced by others.

"Get 'em off! Get 'em off!" she said as she hopped.

Justin snapped into action, grabbing, and swiping at the figures on her legs. He succeeded in knocking a few off, only to have new ones fill in the gaps. The toys began crossing her studded belt and crawled up her hoodie. A couple toys hanging off her body swung knives at Justin's hands, cutting thin lines of pain and blood across his skin. As he fought with the toys, a group of soldiers wound black string around Cam's shins. Panic clawed and chewed on Justin's nerves.

The grumble of tank treads on concrete pierced his concentration. Armored vehicles positioned themselves a few feet away, raising their cannons. Ignoring the toys crawling on her, he wrapped his arms around her and dragged her away.

The concussive blast boomed.

Justin felt the bass thump in his bones. His hands shot up to his ears. As soon as he let go of Cam, she fell. Four pencil-sized darts stuck out of her chest. Blood stained her hoodie a darker shade of black. Motion caught his eyes; the action figures were loading the tanks' cannons with another round of artillery.

Staring down the barrel of their weapons, it didn't take much to figure out who was their next target. Two thoughts burned through Justin at lightning speed. Leave Cam behind or face getting blasted.

He reached for Cam.

The action figures swarmed her like ants on a corpse. Beneath the plastic wave, her arms and legs moved as if underwater. They didn't notice or care, taking their time to tie down her arms. Black strings the size of boot laces were already around her torso. The clang of hammers striking nails, the crunch of breaking cement increased as more soldiers went to work. The toys not binding her were pinching, pulling, and hacking at exposed skin. Blood welled up in the wounds, bits of flesh flaking off her. Angry rosy marks in the shape of small hands marred her face and arms.

It took him a moment to notice the soldiers sneaking toward him. Their knives and guns, the manic grins molded on their faces, their determined steps menaced him. They forced him back from his friend. The cannons traced his movements, keeping him in their sights.

A group of ninja figures, carrying knives and swords, slipped out of the shadows and slunk up to Cam's face.

"Motherfucker," he said as a tank fired, forcing him to duck and back away.

In one swift move, a ninja pierced one of Cam's eyes. Runny white slime dripped down her cheeks. As she screamed, four black-clad warriors jumped into her mouth. Others grabbed her lips and yanked them open. Muffled cries snuck through the plastic bodies crowding her throat. A few toys punched and shook her teeth. She tremored as blood sprayed out of her mouth. Cam strained against her binds as one succeeded in tearing a tooth out of her gums. It tossed it, sending it clattering across the miniature road. Justin crawled forward and another tank fired, the dart grazing his ear. Two ninjas hacked at his hands, keeping him back. Movement on top of Cam pulled his focus, it was enough to make his stomach squirm. The ninja on her face waltzed to her uninjured eye, raising its blade. Justin heard the squelch, saw the eye deflate. The toy used its sleeve to wipe the goo off. While she howled, the gang in her mouth disappeared down her throat.

Faint squishy sounds emanated out of her as her neck bulged. He thought he saw her hoodie jump up in random places. She rocked and moaned. Milky tears dripped from empty eye sockets. Blood trickled out of her ears, down the sides of her mouth. Bumps the size of golf balls formed on her stomach moments before toy daggers popped out. They sawed openings through her skin, allowing hooded figures to appear in the wound. Curtains of blood flowed down her torso, puddling on the road. Cam's movements slowed, as more weapons tore through flesh and cloth along her torso. Ninjas climbed out of her, dark ichor lubricating their escape.

The soldiers intensified their attacks against Justin's hands. His tear-filled eyes made it difficult to strike any of the toys. Curses shot out of his mouth as he crawled backwards. The image of Cam's lifeless body stained his thoughts. Sanity frayed in tattered strips.

Mentally pushing through a void growing inside, he bellowed to Vince, pleading with him that he had good news about getting out.

"Maybe? I don't know. It's something at least," Vince said.

The tanks rolled over Cam's desiccated corpse. Ruby-stained tracks marked their path. The town receded; fake trees brushed against his legs as he crept backwards. When his feet hit the wall, he felt like a cornered rat as he faced down the tanks.

"This way, quick!" Vince said from Justin's left.

Standing, he realized how less threatening the vehicles appeared. Anger bubbled in his stomach, and he floated out of his body. He observed from above as he stomped on tanks. Plastic crunched under his boots, until there were only broken pieces surrounding him.

Justin came back to reality and found Vince on his knees a few paces away waving for him to hurry. His friend pointed into a rectangular hole on the wall near the ground. Warm air wafted out. Next to Vince was a bent piece of metal grating.

"It's the best we've got," he said.

"Fuck it, let's go!"

The metal tunnel had enough room for the two remaining friends to crawl through. Vince scrambled ahead while Justin stuck the cover back on. The hurt and pain from seeing Cam die became a smoggy cloud of truth in his skull.

We're going to die here.

Track 13

Heat radiated through the air vent. Justin's brain pounded against his skull like a sludgy doom drummer. Ahead of him Vince slowed, groaning about his back. The safety pins on his leather jacket scratched against metal in an agonizing screech. Just almost asked where they were going, but decided he didn't care.

Evil toys haunted his thoughts. Each one carrying an absurd nightmarish death. Was it better than what he had beyond the factory's walls? There was nothing out there for him now. All he had were his friends, and he'd basically killed all of them. So, what did it matter if the toys did the same to him?

What about Vince?

What about him?

Do you want all of your friends to die? Can you at least save one of them?

"Hey, Vince. Stop for a minute." Justin sunk down.

"Fuck. Yeah. Okay." Vince crawled back and sat next to Justin.

"What the fuck are we doing? Do you think we'll get

out of here?" Justin slapped the wall, the sound bouncing through the vent. "How the fuck did this happen? Goddammit, Cam is dead."

"Dude. It fucking sucks." Vince stared ahead. "I had no fucking clue it'd be like this. I thought it'd just be another shitty factory, maybe with some broken toys and shit. It's like a damn nightmare."

"God, I wish. I wish I'd wake the fuck up and be passed out in the alley by Green Top. I'd be so friggin' happy to feel that dirty ass brick road digging into my back."

"Oh man, I know it." Vince turned to face Justin. "You know, I felt the same way you felt about them all leaving, right?"

Justin opened his mouth, but nothing came out. He assumed Vince didn't care about anyone. If he was being honest, he didn't know why Vince hung around with them, other than having similar tastes in music. Why was he telling him this now?

"I might not have acted like it, but I always had fun hanging out with you all. I know I'm a bastard and sometimes I hate it. In my head I tell myself not to act that way, but it just sorta happens." Vince punched his thigh twice. "Fuck, they were going to leave us, someone had to take the piss out of them. And how the hell were you or I supposed to know what the fuck was happening here?"

Conflict hollowed Justin's stomach. He'd played with the idea that as soon as his friends left, Vince would disappear. The guy could be a major asshole, and his shady shit terrified Justin. But he would have gone along with it if it meant not being alone. Now, hearing all of this, he wondered if he and Vince were more alike than he realized.

"I know. I just…" Justin squeezed his fists until he could have made diamonds. "I don't know."

Only the whisper of air coming through the shaft listened to them.

Justin glanced at Vince. "Dude, we'll get through this. But first, we need to figure out where the fuck this leads."

"Shit, some place Challis probably didn't plan on anyone going."

"That's probably good, means there won't be any damn toys." Justin wiped his nose. "Let's jump out of the next vent and figure out what to do then."

Vince stuck his hand out and Justin took it, they nodded before Vince crawled ahead.

———

"Oh my god, do you see that?" Vince said.

The vent filled with the thuds of their scrambling toward a glow ahead of them. The source of light came from a grate on the bottom of the duct. Fresh air wafted in. Vince lifted a leg and slammed it against the vent until it popped out.

"Shit, fucking wait one second!" Justin said.

"Why?"

"Because we don't know what might be out there."

Vince rocked, moving his head closer to the opening. He kept glancing between Justin and the space, his eyes burning with impatience. No killer toys or horrible monsters showed themselves. Justin's bowels twisted, his nerves thrummed, his limbs ready to be free. Vince sucked in a deep breath and jumped.

There was a thud, then he called out, "It's fine, come on."

Knowing the only escape would be through this hole, he dropped down.

Track 14

At first, he wondered if they'd entered a different building. Instead of crazy colors, toys, and bizarre rooms, he saw piss yellow walls, dirty fluorescent lights within ceiling tiles, and rooms upon rooms. A slight lemony scent mingled with a pungent earthy aroma.

"Fuck, this is probably the weirdest thing we've seen so far," Justin said.

"Where the hell do you think we are? I mean we are definitely off whatever tour Challis had planned." Vince wandered, scanning the openings leading into similar rooms.

A terrible and hilarious thought came to Justin's mind. He snickered, then broke out laughing.

Concern scrunching Vince's eyebrows. "Uh, dude?"

"What if this was some fucked up part of the contest? Like, did Challis have any office toys or dress up clothes?"

"I don't think so. Come on man, I can't fucking take care of you and me."

Justin shuffled toward a wall; sadness filled in the spaces the mirth had been. Vince was right. He had to hold it together. Some circular indentations in the carpeting, along with grease stains pulled at his attention.

Of course, Challis wouldn't make office toys, that'd be too boring.

Pointing at Vince, he nodded. "You're right, sorry. And I think you're onto something, I bet this is probably their back office. Maybe they didn't want the cops or someone finding whatever they were doing, so they cleared the area out."

A trace of fear crept up Justin's spine as they studied the different paths. Each room mirrored the last one.

"Where do you think we should go now?" Vince said.

Justin searched for an answer while picking some dirt from his neck. From the depths of his mind floated Cam's eyeless face and he lost track of everything. In this mental darkness his thoughts led to the fact he had no idea what they should do. He released a shaky breath.

"Let's go this way for a bit." He motioned with his head toward the opening next to him. "Maybe we'll spot something. I mean, if this was where the office people worked, they had to get in here, right? Maybe there's another entrance."

They walked.

And walked.

Justin limped and Vince rubbed his legs as they passed through the countless rooms piling up behind them. Every once in a while, he thought he heard another set of footsteps, or his skin would prickle with the feeling of being watched. Each time, he'd stop and check, finding nothing. They could have been on a treadmill, never going anywhere.

Vince stopped at an opening Justin had ignored. "Holy shit, look at this."

"Let me guess, it's another room? Maybe with this crappy yellow all over its walls?"

"Dude, just get the fuck over here."

Shuffling, he reached Vince, and his jaw dropped. "Fuckin A."

They stared at a long wide hall with several passageways. Gray walls and carpeting replaced the beige monotony. Half of the fluorescent lights had gone out, creating deep pockets of shadows.

"Maybe we've found the executive side, or a way out," Vince said.

The emptiness of the space thrummed on Justin's nerves. The need to tell Vince about the feeling of being watched, the extra footsteps he heard, the possibility of something being in there pushed to the forefront of his mind. Doubt crippled this need, guessing Vince would think it was nothing. Besides, if Vince didn't notice any of this, maybe he would be right. *I'm tired and seeing things.*

Vince stopped at the first opening on his left. "What the fuck, come on."

Justin scurried to meet his friend. His eyes flashed over a small conference room and landed on the pile in the middle of the otherwise empty space. A spidery chill crawled over his scalp.

Covering the floor were piles of exploded stuffed animals. Empty skins of bears, rabbits, ducks, dogs, cats, and monsters with too many limbs. Stuffing sat in clumps and clung to sticky marks on the carpet. Light glinted off beady black eyes. The stank of moldering leaves and compost hung in the air. On the other side of the massacre stood a half open door, a few scratches in the nearby walls.

The mechanical show he saw in Challis' office flared in Justin's mind. He imagined the imps breaking out of these cute toys, running havoc in the factory, killing his friends. *Motherfucker, was it all true?*

"I just don't even know anymore." Exhaustion slowed Vince's voice.

Justin rubbed his eyes. "Let's keep going."

The two friends trudged on. They passed a room full of toy wheels. Another room full of plastic guns for action figures. The abandoned pieces reminding Justin of his future. He thought of his friends' bodies left in the factory. Should he come back and recover their bodies? They shouldn't be here. Did he really want to come back after all of this? When he reached the end of the hall, he discovered he was alone.

"Vince?"

Fear rumbled in his stomach. *Where the fuck did he go?*

Standing amongst the gray walls of the empty area, he waited and listened. On his right, static, a rhythmic clicking, and the susurrus of whispers. Justin hustled toward the noise, ready to curse Vince. A short path led to an L-shaped hall with a closed door at the end. Blue light shone through the crack under the door. He thought he saw a shadow pass by.

"Vince, what the fuck are you doing in there?"

Stale air washed over him when he opened the door. A metallic blue glow painted a room slightly bigger than a closet. In front of him was a bank of monitors with dust covered screens projecting images of static or shots of the factory. A strip of butcher paper tacked to a wall was marked up with concentric circles with X's and lines in random places, symbols that looked like a child's made-up language. His grime coated Converse squeaked on the tile floor as he went to a card table covered with pens and papers below the TVs. One screen showed the Toy Room, bubbles floating on the pond. On another was what looked like a life-sized board game with pieces sliding along the squares. A bare room with a big metal door, striped tape around it, and burn marks on the floor filled a screen. At the far end of the monitors was a VCR, a tape stuck in its mouth like a dead tongue.

Without thinking, Justin pushed the cassette in and pressed play.

The screen flickered to life. Black and white images of the factory. A group of five children standing near the entrance in front of Challis in his famous frock coat, top hat, wild hair. Lines and distortion danced across the video. Static filled the screen for a moment before it was replaced with the children running around the Toy Room. It surprised him to see the pond full of clean water, the lack of garbage, and the toys dancing and frolicking through the trees. The children chased after toys, picked them up, hugged them, and kicked them. Nostalgia tugged at Justin's heartstrings. He couldn't believe how magical it looked.

Another jump cut. This time there were only three children. Sadness sat like a rock in his stomach at the sight of frowns and tears on the kids' faces, two of them huddled together. Challis guided them on a blocky train. His movements were frantic, his face animated. Distortion ruined the image, a bright blue screen appeared for a few frames before being replaced with a new scene. One of the boys in a circular pit with a spinning floor. Every time he got on his feet, the movement sent him tumbling down. Tears and panic masked the boy's face as he clawed at the slick walls. A gigantic pendulum covered in spikes lowered into view and swung around the pit. The child let out a silent scream, crawling away from the rotating weapon. It only took a moment for the spikes to puncture the boy's body, dragging him along the floor. Black blood splattered the stark white pit. The boy twitched, one of his shoes fell off.

He wanted to walk away. Why was he watching this? The screen filled with static before revealing the five children lying on the ground in a circle. A blue and orange imp hopped in the background.

The video went black.

"What the fuck?" Justin said.

He stumbled back from the monitors. His heart jumped like he had been in the mosh pit of a *Rancid* show. Bile scorched his throat. Tears cut streaks down his filthy cheeks. All of the happy memories of playing with the toys, of dreaming about the factory curdled.

A voice broke through the spiraling questions running through his head. "You bastard!"

Was that Vince?

"Fuck," he said as he hustled back into the hall. Thuds and grunts came from down the corridor. Justin ran toward the noise.

Track 15

"...**Y**ou fucking know where it is!"

Where the hell did that come from? Come on Vince help me out here. Justin's focus darted across the half walls, columns, indents in the walls, and smattering of openings surrounding him. He'd almost finished his search when he noticed an opening tucked behind a column. Justin's breath quickened when the voices grew louder.

He crept into the hidden alcove. The acrid scent of sulfur burned his nose as he passed into the new room.

Vince paced, waving his arms. Behind his friend, in a scorch mark-covered cinder block wall, was an oversized red metal door with bolts and a spinning handle like he'd seen on cartoon vaults. A deep humming vibrated his bones. Yellow and black striped tape marked off a wide rectangle on the floor around the door. Scrunched in the righthand corner was a dirty mattress, and a table covered in books and notepads. None of this compared to the tall lanky man wearing a filthy mustard coat, a crooked purple top hat, and houndstooth pants. The man leaned on a splintering cane as he eyed Vince.

"Young man, I'm sorry to disappoint you, but I don't know what you are talking about." The man's voice was raspy as frayed paper, yet a floating singsong quality hid in the sentence. "This area isn't meant for children, it's not safe for you to see the magic that makes the factory tick. It'll ruin your dreams and imagination."

"Holy shit, Challis?" Justin whispered.

Vince smirked, his eyes flashing. "You see, no fucking children here. You can drop the bullshit. We know it's here and you fucking owe us."

Justin cringed. A quick scan didn't exactly point to him having money. If anything, the man was squatting here.

Yet, Justin wondered.

There could be treasure behind the vault-like door if you ignored the sounds of growling and screaming coming from it.

No, none of this is right.

Challis turned, revealing a haggard face full of pock marks, sunken cheeks, and yellowish skin. The old man smiled when his bright violet eyes fell on Justin, revealing gray teeth.

"Welcome to my factory, kiddo! As wonderful as it is to see young ones again, I really have to reiterate you shouldn't be here."

Justin stared at Challis, a ball of barbed wire growing in his mind. This couldn't be the same man that had created so many wonderful toys, magical memories for so many children. "How? How are you here?"

"Well, where else would I be dreaming up fantastical toys for you?" The frayed quality to his voice begun to disappear, the lilting child-like singsong growing pronounced.

Justin stepped forward, his hands balling tight enough to crack plastic. "You've been hiding here this whole fucking time? What the actual fuck? Our friends died because of your goddamn toys. Why? Why the fuck are your toys alive?"

Challis backed up, glancing at the red door. The smile melted from his face. Metal groaned, ticking rapped in a rhythmic staccato, and the screams grew louder.

Vince joined Justin. "You can drop the fucking act you old bastard. Tell us where the money is and maybe we won't kick the shit out of you."

"I'm so sorry about my toys playing with your friends. None of this was meant to happen. At first, they seemed like the perfect thing for kids, the magic to make the toys live. But they didn't want to stop, they didn't want children to rest. I tried telling them, but they wouldn't listen. I've been trying to hold them back, but they must have found another way to creep in."

Drool slicked Challis' chin. He never blinked. He pulled at his hair. "If you've seen them then it means things are bad."

Challis' mention of *them* sent icy water trickling down Justin's spine. The fake Challis at the front door, the blue and orange figures he saw in the Toy Room, the diorama machine, all pointed to the truth. The imps were real...and they wanted to play. "How? Where's the fucking exit?"

"It's not far from here. You must hurry though." Challis hobbled toward a stack of books. "There's a way out through those rooms, I thought I'd be able to leave and come back when I built this maze, but that was foolish. I promise it'll get you out lickety-split."

Before Challis could help, Vince lunged at him.

"Bullshit! Don't you dare hold out on us!"

Shock tore through Justin. "Come on man, don't do this."

"What's behind the door?" Vince shook the old man. "Is that where you are keeping the money?"

"Dude, give it a rest. Let's get outta here." Justin wrapped an arm around him.

Vince jerked away, his eyes boring into the factory owner. "No. The fucker is holding out. You said it yourself, our friends fucking died here. He owes us three lives for killing them."

Challis' mouth moved, his rancid breath bringing tears to Justin's eyes. "I...I...didn't know there were so many out. I thought I was repeating the spell enough times."

"Fuck you. Your fucking playhouse of nightmares murdered Michelle, Aaron, and Cam. That was their names, the people you took from us. It's your fucking time." Spit flew from Vince's mouth, his face burning red as he jerked the old man around.

The humming in the room increased, vibrating Justin's skull. He got into Vince's eyeline. "Dude, it's okay. They'd want us to get out. This won't bring them back."

"The boy is right; you need to get out." Challis wiggled from Vince's grip and paced. His hands flitted about like spiders as he muttered to himself. "Maybe there's something stronger, maybe I missed something in the spell."

Questions about the imps and whatever spell Challis mentioned bounced around Justin's thoughts. He tried to convince himself he didn't need to know. "Just show us how to leave. Then you can do whatever it is you need to do."

A red glow snuck out between the edges of the door. Inhuman screams grew closer. Dust puffed off the walls.

"Or, how about you come with us? This whole place feels like it's falling apart. Maybe you can tell everyone what happened here?"

The old factory owner stopped, the light surrounding him, his feet at the edge of the yellow and black tape. Strength emboldened his voice. "Thank you for the offer my child, but I told you I can't leave. No, you need to go and tell everyone there's nothing here. No one can ever come back."

Vince sprang at Challis. The two tumbled to the ground. There was a loud crack, and the man groaned, then Vince began raining fists down on him. The room filled with sickening smacks and crunching of bone. The old man strived to protect himself but was outmatched by the younger and scrappier kid. Justin rushed over to stop Vince. If he killed the factory owner, Challis wouldn't be able to show them how to get out. How long could they wander and hope they'd stumble upon the exit? Especially with the threat of the imps. Justin had no question now on where they came from, he knew they were behind that door. Vince shoved him aside and continued the assault.

"Vince!"

Justin tried again. Besides Challis helping them escape, they could probably turn him in. Letting him live here while their friends had died, those kids died, wasn't right. Maybe this is why he survived, maybe this is what he could do with his life. If he could convince Vince to stop and see reason, they might still have time. Then he saw the blood and the glazed look in Challis' eyes.

"Fuck, dude, you killed him."

Track 16

Vince climbed off Challis. He studied his torn knuckles, the ichor splattered on his leather jacket, and recognition washed over him. The old man lay there, his face a mess of red blood and white bone. The humming and crackle increased. Justin glared at Vince and felt sick.

"What the fuck are we going to do now? He was going to show us the way out."

Vince wiped his hands on his pants and glanced at the door. "The bastard said it was close. But first, let's get what he owes us."

The ruby glow intensified, static energy gained mass and slipped through the door as Vince crossed the tape on the floor. For a moment, Justin swore the wall bulged, and his balls shrank. "What the fuck dude? There's no money in there."

"Don't tell me you were buying his bullshit."

Heat radiated from the walls. Guttural groans and scratching filled the room. Vince grabbed the round spindly lock. Warning bells screamed in Justin's head.

Somewhere behind the noise came a quiet moan. Movement caught Justin's attention. Vince spun the handle.

Challis shuddered. Quiet words trickled out of his mouth. "Don't open it."

Justin's breath caught in his throat. Did he imagine hearing the old man? He knelt and gently put a finger next to Challis' neck. He had a general idea on how to check for life, and maybe a bit of first aid, having dealt with getting the shit kicked out of himself before. There was a slight pulse.

"You mustn't go in there."

"We have to get you some help. How do we get out of here?"

"Don't worry about me. Worry about him. They won't let him live."

The door creaked, and a cacophony of discordant screams exploded out. A heavy feeling of dread sat on Justin's chest. His attention shot to his friend as a bright red light escaped the opening. He shielded his eyes, only getting a glimpse of his friend's silhouette. Gusts of wind carrying the rotten smells of decayed meat and rancid vegetables flew into the space. He didn't hear Vince say he found the money, didn't hear him cry out, nothing but wails and the buzzing hum.

"What the fuck is happening?"

"It's the gate. They had been waiting for me to grow weak, for someone to open the door. The full force of them will join the others if you don't do something quick. Once they are out..."

"Like what? What the hell can I do?"

Challis grabbed Justin's arm with a frail hand. His eyes were bloodshot, the pupils swirling as if being pulled in a drain. "You need to close it. You need to stay here and help me keep up the spell."

The wind died down, replaced with the moist hot breath of someone standing too close. The buzzing increased until it became palpable. He tried to understand what Challis was talking about. All he knew was his last friend had gone through, and he didn't want to be alone.

"I'm not going to close that door with Vince in there. Fuck that. I'm going in."

Challis clucked and offered a pathetic smile. "You can't. He's gone. If you go in there you won't be coming out either. You need to be here. If I die and no one replaces me, nothing will stop them from leaving."

This was all too much for Justin. He stood and shuffled toward the door.

"I have to get my friend."

The old man struggled onto his elbows. Red drool dribbled out of his mouth. He closed his eyes. "It's too late to help him. Please. This is more important than anything. The most important thing you'll ever do."

The crimson light faded. Justin squinted at the opening. Could he let his last friend die alone? If there had been money, Vince would have already come running out with cash. Was Challis telling him the truth? Would he find imps tearing into his buddy, and would they attack him next?

He went to the threshold.

"Vince, are you okay?"

Try as he might, he couldn't spot Vince. He could just make out a square of shiny greens, browns, and yellows through the smoke and mist swirling in front of him. Insects chittered, animals screeched, and rhythmic drumming kept the beat. All of it reminded him of something he'd seen before but couldn't place where.

Back away, close the door.

The square pushed through the fog, growing until it filled his vision.

Alien plants with leaves the size of houses faded into view. An earthy scent wafted out and reminded him of a forgotten compost pile. Unseen things skittered about, claws clicking. Heavy pressure pulled at him, squeezing bones and internal organs. Voices chanted in unknown languages.

It's that scene from the machine in Challis' office. Fuck, he really did go there.

Justin wept as he stumbled. A dry, bony hand snatched at his arm. He stared into the face of a blue imp. Molded orange hair bunched around its head, bulging emerald eyes glittered with mischief, its thin nose almost touching his own nose, a broad lipless mouth sneered revealing tiny, pointed teeth sticking out of throbbing black gums. His bowels loosened, warming his pants with urine. A sickly-sweet voice invaded his mind. "Come in, we can give your friends a new life. We've been in humans before, it's painless. You can have everything you want. You just have to help us play with the children."

Behind the imp, he caught the sight of five diminutive silhouettes huddled under leaves. One of them seemed to be full of stuffing, a girl of porcelain wearing a frilly dress, another made of shiny plastic with exposed joints, the third child was a blocky robotic insect covered in human skin, a boy whose frame had been shrunk and stretched into a horrible monster reminiscent of one of the bad guys from the Shark Commandos.

Justin screamed.

Something howled in anger, followed by a thunderous clap. The world shook. Sulfur and death clouded the air. Shadows slithered, crawled, and marched toward him.

Where was Vince?

He kicked the monster, his Converse connecting with its gut. It squealed. Screams, growls, and wet slurpy noises responded.

"Vince!" The racket swallowed his voice. Tears streamed down his cheeks. Was it selfish to leave him? Or would it be better to stop these terrible beings from escaping? There was no real choice. Bowing his head, he promised Vince he'd find some way to save him. He backed from the fantastic sight and reached for the door.

Pulling with all his might, his attempt to slam the door shut was stopped when a pair of impish blue hands shot through.

Track 17

"You motherfucking piece of shit!" Justin screamed as he fought with the monster.

For being all skin and bones, it was strong. His limbs quaked. Panic deepened until it consumed his mind. The opening increased. The pair of hands was joined by two, three more. Laughter bubbled.

A voice cut through Justin's terror. "You can do it, buddy."

"Vince! You're alive!" Sparks of energy popped in Justin's muscles. "Can you make it through?"

"Naw, man. Close the door, don't let the fuckers through."

In Justin's mind he heard Michelle and Aaron encouraging him. Telling him to stop this from happening to anyone else. He felt Cam next to him, her hands next to his. He choked back a sob.

"We'll be with you," she said.

Squeezing every bit of strength he had, he planted his feet and pushed. Behind him, unfamiliar words coughed out of an old man's lips. The imps and beasts squealed. The door shook. The veins on Justin's neck and arms bulged. *Guys, I'll do something good, I promise.*

With one last thrust, the door clicked shut.

———

"I made some poor decisions in my earlier life. My only hope was to give children happiness. But that was twisted and used against me. I've taken on the penance of protecting them now." Challis' body tremored; scarlet stained his graying chin.

Justin sat on the floor, a husk of himself. His brain felt like a glob of wet paper towels. He listened to Challis tell him about the gate, about the spells. It all sounded insane.

"You've seen what was in there. You resisted them. I think you might be strong enough to keep them at bay. It's a great responsibility, and not something I'd wish on anyone..."

"Fucking hell."

He wanted to say no. He wanted to run and keep on running. But he had made a promise. No one deserved to face what was in there. Even if he had a future to go to outside the factory, could he? No. There was nothing in the world but wasting his life at a dead-end job, wishing for the past. But now, with his friends' bodies here? That his friend was behind that door. No, this was his purpose now. A loftier purpose than anything he could imagine.

The growling and humming hung in the background.

"So, what do I need to do?" Justin said.

Challis grimaced before pulling his lips back in an attempt at a smile. The dirt on his face flaked off. "I knew as soon as I saw you that you were special. You will have to take my place here. It's the only way to keep the gate closed.

"But, I am so sorry for this. You won't ever be able to leave. This is going to be your life. Your sacrifice, however, will be protecting the whole world."

Challis slowly got up and walked to the table. He showed Justin the books. Walked him through the spells and incantations that needed to be muttered every day. The old factory owner tremored and hacked through it all. Justin thought about music, hanging out in bars with his friends to see new bands. It'd all be gone, forever. As he stared at Challis, sadness fell upon him, this was his future.

Yet, he felt a familiar presence, the imaginary weight of four pairs of hands on him.

"You'll constantly have to be on your guard. Your world is now this room, this factory. I'm sorry about that."

Justin searched for what to say, his friends in the back of his mind, encouraging, joking, singing punk songs. "Well, let's get this fucking show started."

THE END

Acknowledgments

Man, here we are, round two of *...And Out Come the Toys*. It's been a bit of a crazy ride getting this thing out. I won't bore you with the details, let's just say this is the version I envisioned, and I'm stoked you read it.

There's a ton of kick ass people that helped and supported me with this book. I'll try not to make the list too long.

I want to thank Matt Blairstone for the killer cover, and dealing with all of my random questions.

Sam Richard for offering advice, listening to me whine, and the layout.

Alex Woodroe helped with the back cover and that's rad!

Betty Rocksteady for absolutely nailing it with the logo, I'm so happy I finally got to work with her.

Nicole Lightner, Kathleen Palm, and Thomas Joyce, thank you for being first readers and giving me a ton of great advice.

Special thanks go to my family and friends. You all put up with my insanity and wackiness. Thank you for humoring me whenever I bring up some strange idea or twist the things you love into something horrible. You all keep me going and not become some sort of hermit.

And my Staring into the Abyss crew. Richard Gerlach and Villimey Mist, you both are family and my Saturdays are better for being able to record with you.

Finally, Roald Dahl and Mel Stuart for making Willy Wonka & The Chocolate Factory, and Rancid for ...And Out Come the Wolves. These two things have been a part of my life for a long time and had such a huge impact on me.

Since I've got you here, and since I used to love digging through the shout outs of punk CDs, I figured I could do that too. So here's some rad people you'll dig:

Carson Winter, Charlen Elsby, Danger Slater, Nicole Cushing, Matthew Mitchell, Patrick Barb, Ryan Bradley, Laura Bolger, Christopher Hawkins, Maria Dong, Alex Ebenstein, Anthony Engebretson, Tamika Thompson, Max Booth, Michael Dixon, L.C. von Essen, Joe Koch, Kyle Winkler, Laurel Hightower, Orrin Grey, Jonathan Raab, Ivy Grimes.

About the Author

Matt Brandenburg is a horror writer living next to a moldy pumpkin patch in Kalamazoo, Michigan. He is the author of ...*And Out Come the Toys*. You can find his short stories in *34 Orchard*, *No Lives Left*, *Novus Monstrum*, and *Tales to Terrify*. He is also a cohost on the podcast Staring Into The Abyss. When he's not writing cartoonish horror, he is usually listening to horror movie scores, watching goofy movies, or playing with Lego. Find him on Bluesky and his website matt-brandenburg.com

www.ingramcontent.com/pod-product-compliance
Lightning Source LLC
Chambersburg PA
CBHW061125100726
47911CB00013B/689